OUTBACK ARRIVAL

SUZI LOVE

OUTBACK ARRIVAL

A contemporary medical romance with mystery set in an outback Australian hospital.

A city nurse follows the doctor she loves to the Australian outback town where he manages his family cattle property and recovers from an ambulance accident.

Kristie takes a job at the local hospital, but when she realizes she is pregnant her lover cannot accept that the baby is his, having been manipulated by people he trusted.

But in order to gain his greatest wish, a wife and family, Alex must chose between Kristie, a dedicated nurse and his passionate lover, and his closest family. Because if Kristie leaves the outback, she will take his heart with her.

Outback Arrival

eBook: 9780992345662

Print: 9780992345679

Copyright © 2026 by Suzi Love

All Rights Reserved.

For permission requests, please contact:

Suzi Love, 258/ 52 University Way, Sippy Downs, Queensland, 4556, Australia.

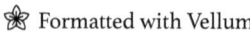 Formatted with Vellum

1

'No, no, no! Bodies don't stand up and walk out of hospitals.'

'I'm real sorry, Nurse Kristie.' The weather beaten grounds-man shuffled his feet in front of her office desk, distress adding a decade to his sixty something years. 'Looked ever 'where. Can't find it.'

'This can't be happening, Joey. A corpse cannot just disappear. Somebody must have noticed something.'

'Sure ain't sometin´ no normal person'd tuck un'erneath their arm. Walk out with, when visitors go 'ome.'

Kristie adopted the calm and confident demeanor that had helped her tackle hundreds of emergency room dramas without showing a moment of panic. Casualty nurses joked that no matter how many crazy things you'd dealt with, something stranger was always about to walk in your door. Or in today's case, walk out of the morgue's door.

She hauled in a deep breath, while mentally chastising herself for not making more time to attend yoga classes, for Joey's sake if not her own. She faked a confident smile. 'We have to find his body, Joey. Quickly. Before the board's fusspots hear what's happened. Or we'll have them arriving, en masse, and breathing down our necks.'

When she'd arrived four weeks earlier, the majority of the board members had welcomed her with open arms. Enticing an experienced nurse away from a city hospital to a remote outback town didn't happen every day and the town had seen them as heroes saving their stretched outback health system. The few remaining few board members, however, were old-fashioned, staid, and highly suspicious of her motives. Perhaps they'd seen too many young girls move west in the hope of hooking a young station owner and living what used to be a wealthy, fly in and fly out lifestyle for many sheep graziers. But while Australia had once ridden on the sheep's back, things had changed dramatically in rural towns. Any family members still working their properties were so busy and money-strapped that visits to the local town were merely a fortnightly stock up of food and fencing goods. If roads were okay, maybe they'd snatch a couple of hours at the pub for a meal, a beer, and an update on livestock prices.

Kristie had learned to be vigilant at work and circumspect when off duty. During her three months' probation as Director of Nursing, she couldn't afford any slip ups or she wouldn't be contracted for a permanent position, no matter how desperate rural towns were to keep medical staff.. Those board members, the ones lacking a sense of humor, would be horrified that a recently deceased member of their small community had mysteriously disappeared from the hospital's morgue. Although morgue was a loose term for a brick shed which housed a refrigerator, a work bench, and was supposedly cooled by a temperamental air-conditioner. Misplacing a body, without any of her rostered staff noticing, would be classified by the board as her first mistake, a huge mistake.

Joey shifted awkwardly in his enormous, old work boots. 'Someone hacked the lock right outta the door. Made off with Wilhelm's body while I was busy helpin' with the men's showers.'

'Who'd do that?'

'Dunno. Crazy man, that's for sure.'

'What about the morgue sign out book?'

'Nothin' there. Jocelyn signed when she checked the thermostat, six this mornin'. Everything good. Same last night. Maxine checked.'

'So in less than two hours,' Kristie said as she paced behind her desk, 'someone cut the lock out of a solid wooden door and carried away a body. A very large man's body. And nobody heard or saw anything.'

'Whoever them people that took Wilhelm, been very clever. Six o'clock in mornin' everyone is busy. Cookin' breakfast. Havin' showers. Nurses too busy to look out back. Nobody takes no notice of Morgue anyways, 'cept to check fridge workin'. Don't want no trouble. Not like that other time.'

With a premonition of doom, Kristie asked the obvious question. 'What happened that other time?'

'Very hot time of year. Few summers ago. Had a death. Terrible thing that, when someone dies before—'

'Joey, I don't have time for that now. Tell me about the morgue.'

'Fridge fan seized. Trouble was, generator motor sounded like goin' good. Making usual racket. Young relief nurse from city, she smelled—'

Sweat droplets trickled down the back of Kristie's neck. Her head swam and her vision blurred. She plopped back down into her desk chair and sucked in more deep breaths.

'Enough, Joey. I get the picture.' She flapped a hand towards her groundsman and hoped he'd leave before her heaving stomach disgraced itself.

He shook his head, making his wiry grey curls bob around his furrowed brow. 'Sure hope you ain't gonna be one of them squeamish city nurses.'

She forced another smile. 'Certainly not.'

Her stomach, normally stout despite the extreme sights and smells of an emergency room, was at odds with itself today. She glanced past Joey's head to where her reflection showed in the half-open glass door. cringed at her reflection. Pasty complexion and dark-ringed eyes. She looked more like a tormented panda than a capable nursing sister. And she couldn't succumb to the flu bug flying around town, as half her staff were already curled up in their beds miserable and unable to work.

'Some nurses, when they come to the bush, they get mad when crazy things 'appen. But that's the way of the outback. Things go wrong. Bush people fix 'em.'

'So,' Kristie said, swallowing hard, 'after the incident with the broken fan, the sign in book was started.'

'Yep. Not that many people die here. But morgue's locked up tight. Thermostat checked six in mornin', six at night. All proper.'

She paced back and forth across her office, five steps each way. 'Too risky to steal the key from my office. Better to hack into the door. But to move Wilhelm, they would have needed a trolley. Or a truck.'

'No trolleys gone. Could have used the hearse. Ring Dan at the Council. Town undertaker. Digs graves. Drives hearse for burials.'

Joey shuffled off, after dropping his bombshell into what he considered her capable lap. For a good five minutes, Kristie leaned back against the wall and stared at her desk and at the phone that she didn't want to pick up. First, she tackled the lesser the two devils and dialed the police station.

The over-zealous constable prattled on for a full ten minutes. A missing man, alive or dead, was an unusual and exciting event. He thanked her profusely, as if she'd engineered a body-snatching to save him from mundane paper work and give him a real crime to investigate. He promised to verify the whereabouts of the hearse and personally door knock every house within spying distance of the hospital.

Kristie summoned her optimism and gathered it around her like a child wrapped in its cuddle blanket. This was a closely-knit rural town and the locals' main pastime was gossiping. Surely someone would fill the constable's ears with any comings and goings they'd spotted around the hospital grounds. Surely they'd have Wilhelm's body back in the morgue before morning tea.

She stared at the phone again. Her hands shook and her body felt overheated and clammy. She stood in front of the clunky fan and lifted the hem of her work shirt, flapping it several times to cool her sticky body. Procrastination wasn't her normal method for tackling problems. She preferred a head on approach. Better to get unwanted tasks over and done with. She reached out and plucked up the receiver.

Doctor Alex Ryan's return to Undulla, his family's wide-spread cattle station, had been the talk of the town for the past few weeks. After his leg plaster had been removed, Alex had emerged from his property only on the days the physiotherapist was in town. He'd been too preoccupied with the therapy that was strengthening his muscles to even call in at the main hospital buildings and catch up with any of the long-term staff who were his friends.

With some skillful maneuvering, Kristie avoided the area around the therapies rooms and the long covered walkway that attached it to the hospital. Yet she regularly heard about his progress. She knew his arm had regained full extension and mobility. Knew he was driving himself hard and long to ensure his leg regained full movement. But until today she'd managed to avoid a face to face meeting.

Now, ready or not, the time had arrived for the confrontation her mind dreaded, yet her heart had yearned for. The simple truth was that she'd missed seeing him, hearing his voice, or being with him. She dialed Alex's number. Butterflies executed gymnastic leaps in her still roiling stomach.

She didn't deceive herself. that she wasn't ecstatic about seeing Alex again in all his flesh and blood glory, but she'd expected far longer to prepare. Planned on spending several weeks without him around to work out exactly what she wanted from him, or even what he might read into her sudden appearance in his life again after the way she'd treated him before.

Damn! Perhaps the situation was too complicated to ever unravel and no good would come of her being here. Still, no one had ever accused her of being a coward. Impulsive, headstrong, and a tiny bit too stubborn on occasion, But she'd never run from her problems and she wouldn't now. Despite Dr Alex Ryan being six foot two inches of masculine and muscled problem. Dealing with him would be as difficult as following a lion back to its lair and attempting to rationalize with it.

Her call to Undulla rang and rang and rang. She swallowed hard, forcing down the lump that threatened to block her throat and counted off the seconds until she could legitimately replace the receiver in its cradle. Her thoughts drifted to other cradles where chubby babies rocked to and fro under the watchful eyes of contended parents. She'd swallowed her pride, followed her heart, and come to this town to try to convince Alex to take another chance on forging a future together.

Lately, her thoughts ran in never-ending circles, especially in her bed at night when she was alone, and lonely. The axis anchoring every one of those wearying thoughts was Alex Logan. She imagined that falling, exhausted, into her bed would end any girlish and fanciful dreams but even after long and busy days trying to prove herself in her new position, she tossed and turned and worried if she'd done the right thing. Along with her decision to move to the outback, she'd vowed to stop any more useless 'what ifs'.

Secrets and misconceptions had driven a wedge as big as semi-trailer between she and Alex only days after she'd begun to play childish mind games. If she came to Alex's town, if she met his friends and town's people, would they believe her? The last thing she'd intended was to hurt a man they'd known all their lives, a doctor they loved and respected. Now she faced an enormous task. Convincing an entire town that she'd been protecting her brother, and Mike's, when she'd hidden things from Alex. Apart from persuading a stubborn and heart-scarred surgeon to finally listen to the truth.

Despite knowing Alex had, once again, erected a protective shell around his heart, she was determined to at least speak to him, face to face, and explain. Even if Alex never forgave her enough to resume their close relationship, she couldn't bear to imagine him living the rest of his life with his defenses erected against all women. God knew Alex had plenty of reasons to mistrust women and their motives.

She'd visited him in hospital after his accident and witnessed his determination to not only prove that boys from the bush were a tough breed, but to recover enough so he could return to the operating theatres.

Alex had been raised as a Logan, a cattle baron, and a man who stood strong and made his mark in the vast Australian outback. But now Kristie prayed she could reach the other side of Alex, the more sentimental and loyal family man. He'd suffered so much recently, physically and mentally, and those hardships and disillusionments had left deep scars. Convincing Alex that she wanted to stand beside him, no matter which path he chose in the future, wasn't going to be an easy task.

She jumped up and away from the phone, stretching the cord to its fullest length so she wouldn't be tempted to slam down the receiver. She resumed her pacing behind the desk and waited for her call to ring out. Perhaps if she waited they would have recovered Wilhelm's body and she could delay speaking to Alex for another week. She was about to hang up when a deep voice shimmered across the line.

'Alex Ryan.'

Her knees turned to jelly and she plopped into the chair. Gripping the edge of her desk, she stuttered, 'Ah ... ah ... Alex ...'

'This is Alex.' He sounded curt and impatient. Exactly the way he'd been on surgical rounds if he discovered that a medical student or nurse had made a stupid mistake because they hadn't taken the time to thoroughly investigate a patient's history. Alex was an infinitely-patient educator of new medical students and nurses, but was intolerant of staff whose sloppy work endangered a patient under his care. Worst of all for Kristie's current situation, he was noted for withholding forgiveness until the perpetrator of a dangerous mistake proved, time and again, that they'd learned to take far more care with patient's lives.

'This is Kristie.' It took her another moment to gather the courage to add, 'Kristie Donaldson.' The silence lengthened. Anxiety, or guilt, compelled her to add, 'Kristie from Brisbane.'

'I know who you are.' The ice in his voice would freeze the morgue faster than the ancient generator they relied upon. 'the only question is, what do you want?'

'I'm ...uh...ringing to tell you about a problem.' Another deafening silence. 'At the hospital.'

'Hospital?' As she'd expected, he sounded confused. 'Which hospital?'

Her voice dropped to a whisper. 'The Valley Hospital.'

'Dinosaur Valley?' His horror was evident. 'You're here? At my Shire hospital?'

'Yes.' She paused to steady her voice. 'I'm Acting Director of Nursing for three months.' She waited for the explosion.

'What? Where's Dulcie?'

Butterflies flapped their wings in her stomach and she clutched herself with her free hand. She didn't have the time, or the energy, to fight off a stomach flu.

'Dulcie's daughter broke her leg so Dulcie took emergency leave to look after her grandchildren. She may not return at all.'

'Why didn't someone tell me before this?' Despite being a good distance from him, his barked question made Kristie jump.

Bile rose in her throat. She scrambled for a plausible excuse and willed her stomach to settle. She wasn't about to reveal that she'd convinced the other board members to keep the terms of her appointment quiet until she'd settled in, passed her three month evaluation period, and her future appointment was decided.

'I ... uh ... I don't really know.' Her heart pounded and her face felt hot and flushed. Thank goodness she wasn't confronting him in person. She was a hopeless liar and could never keep a poker face.

'Huh! Don't bother concocting some far-fetched story to tell me. I can hear your brain cogs turning from here. I'll get to the bottom of that later. For now, just explain why you're ringing me?'

'You're the on-call contact for the board this week. And as I said, we have a small incident at the hospital.'

'How small?'

'I guess it's not really small. More a large problem. Six feet tall, to be accurate.'

'What the hell are you talking about?'

'We seem to be...uh... missing a body.' She twisted the phone cord around her fingers and braced herself.

'A body. A dead body?'

'Yes. Mr. Wilhelm Schmidt.'

'And where was Mr. Schmidt's body?'

'In the morgue. Waiting to go on the train today to the coast. The Coroner in Rockhampton will be doing a Post Mortem.'

'Hmm. So Wilhelm hasn't seen a doctor recently?'

'Not for at least two years.'

'Wasn't it locked? The morgue, I mean?'

'Of course it was locked.' She tried to ignore his accusing tone. 'All the security checks were done and signed for. Joey said whoever took Wilhelm used a saw to cut the entire lock out of the door.'

'Hell! Have you notified the police?'

'Sergeant Brooks already knows. His constable will be here within the hour to do photographs and fingerprints.'

'Fine. I should be there by then.'

'Alex—'

'No! Doctor Ryan is better. The last thing we need is for word to spread in the town that we've met before.'

'Ah, about that—'

'Oh, good grief. You haven't actually had the nerve to tell people —'

'No, no. Not me. But Mike—'

'Despite your best efforts to prevent it, Mike is now happily married and on his honeymoon. Why would he tell anyone about us?'

'Because he knows I'm working here. He unfortunately let the cat out of the bag by telling his family. Who then told other people.'

'Wonderful. Now the whole town knows. And I suppose they also know who you are, or should I say, what you are.'

'No, nobody knows everything. Well, except for us. But I've met a lot of Mike's family. When we worked at the same hospital and when we lived next door to each other.'

'I'm only too well aware,' he paused, his tone dripped icicles, 'to the intimate relationship you shared with Mike.'

'Oooh, you blockhead. You still don't understand anything. Still too stubborn to find out the truth.'

'Perhaps you've forgotten.' Now his words dripped sarcasm. 'I caught the two of you. The morning after Mike's wedding.'

She heard his groan and pictured him as he'd been at the hotel, staring at her as if she'd crawled out from under a rock. Alex's obvious distress didn't please her, although it did give her a small measure of comfort. If he'd been suffering a fraction of the regrets and torment she felt, there may yet be a chance for them to talk and clear up all the confusion. She longed to stay here, to work with him again, and to heal their hurts.

Her mind drifted back to her daydreams of a happily-ever-after and she almost missed what Alex said. 'Something was going on between you. But Mike's a married man who is married to my best friend. So if you've come here to cause trouble, for either of them, I'll make—'

'How dare you threaten me. I tried to explain but you were pig-headed to listen.'

'I didn't need to hear your excuses. I saw you kiss Mike on the day after his wedding.'

'You jumped to your own conclusions and you were so certain that you were correct that you didn't ask for an explanation. Too busy storming off in your customary self-righteous arrogance.'

He hissed in a breath. 'I didn't need to hear your excuses. Don't forget, I've met your type plenty of times before.'

'Oh, yes. We all know you're an expert on love. Monica dumped you so you assume every woman you meet is going to be a bitch like her.'

At his shocked gasp, she realized that she'd once more reacted to his mistrust with anger, not understanding. 'I apologize. That was uncalled for.'

'Forget it. I have.' After a moment's silence, she heard him mutter,

'And I stupidly thought I'd forgotten you.' He sighed. 'Why the hell are you here?'

'The job came up and I wanted to try somewhere different.'

'You had a good job in Brisbane.'

'I needed a change of scenery.'

He snorted. The aggravating man actually snorted while she'd been wracked with remorse because she'd ripped open his old wound. From the moment they'd met, her emotions had been on a roller coaster ride of highs and lows. At present, the lows were deep dark pits.

'Don't tell me,' he said in that same snide tone, 'you were caught with someone else's husband.'

'You bastard. You're jumping to ridiculous conclusions again. You know nothing—'

Her head began to swim and the phone slipped from her grip. It banged against the leg of the desk a couple of times before the receiver came to rest on the floor.

Kristie clutched her stomach. 'Ooooh.' She dry retched several times.

2

Alex's medical senses snapped to full alert. He jerked upright in his office chair and his feet landed with a thud on the floor. He'd heard the phone clatter and could picture it hitting the wooden desk in the Nurse Manager's office at the Valley Hospital. Those moans had sounded like Kristie was in genuine distress. He listened to another series of noises, somewhere between heaves and groans.

'What was that? Are you okay?'

Alex willed Kristie to pick up the phone and talk to him but there was only silence. He cursed his lack of self-control and his unprofessionalism. He'd turned a conversation about a hospital problem into a personal assault on the nurse in charge, though he blamed his uncalled-for reaction on shock.

The last thing he'd expected was a local phone call from Kristie. It had been easy to ignore her persistent phone calls after he'd left Brisbane as he'd been determined to never see, speak to, or think about this woman again. Though running away from everyone and immersing himself in hard physical work on a distant beef property hadn't wiped away his memories.

Kristie now haunted him again, in person, and of all places, in his valley. That first sexy whisper of her voice had brought memories best forgotten flooding into his mind. During their love-making, Kristie hadn't quietly sighed or murmured like any other woman. Oh, no! She'd whimpered, moaned, and then screamed. Loudly, and over and over until the sounds of her enjoyment and her wild noises had settled in the depths of his soul.

For two weeks, they'd wallowed in each other's arms. Catered to the other's wants and needs until they'd drowned in pleasure and given a part of themselves to the other. A part of himself he'd desperately tried to reclaim after they parted. Yet, he still felt hollow with loss.

'Hello, hello, hello.' Something was wrong, very wrong. 'Answer me!'

Someone spoke at last. 'Hello, this is Mary Klein. Who am I talking to?'

'Mary. Thank goodness.'

Mary was one of the hospital's long-term employees. She'd worked there on and off during three pregnancies and while her children were attended the local primary school. Now she worked to pay exorbitant boarding school fees for her three teenagers.

'It's Alex Ryan. I was talking to Kristie Donaldson. I heard some strange noises and Kristie disappeared.'

'Kristie was feeling a little sick. She had to go.'

'Has she got the flu? I heard half the town caught it.'

'It's not my place to say...'

Alex chuckled. Mary was one of the town's biggest gossip, though she was also one of the most generous people in town. Always first to lend a hand to any needy family and as the hospital couldn't function without her local knowledge, her gossiping tendencies were ignored.

'Okay, Mary. What does a little sick mean?'

'Kristie hasn't said anything but I assumed...'

'Assumed what?'

'No, it's not my place to say anything. It's up to Kristie. Although, as a member of the board, I suggest you ask her. Especially if she plans on making this a permanent position.'

'Did she tell you she intends on staying here? In our valley.'

Mary adopted her well-known mothering voice. After Alex's mother had died, Mary had taken him under her wing. And had later done the same for his step siblings. She therefore felt free to voice her opinion on any, and every, subject concerning the Ryan family.

'Now, Alex, just because your fiancée—'

'Ex-fiancée.' He immediately regretted his sharp tone. Mary's habit of reading his mind, and everyone else's in town, meant that more than anyone she knew how much Monica's defection had hurt him.

'Oh, don't worry, I'm very happy that schemer is your ex-fiancée. But because one woman refused to live in our valley, doesn't mean all women dislike living in the outback. I've lived here all my life and wouldn't live anywhere else. Monica wasn't the right type of woman for you, that's for certain.'

Alex shook his head. Twice in one phone conversation he'd been berated over Monica, and by two different women.

'Mary, is Kristie there yet?'

'No. Judging by the last couple of days, she'll be in the bathroom for a while yet.'

'She's really that sick?'

'You'd better stop avoiding the hospital, Alex, and get yourself in here. With you being Kristie's special friend, you should see for yourself.'

Alex mentally ground his teeth. 'I didn't say I was a friend of Nurse Donaldson.'

'Everybody knows you met Kristie at Mike and Jenny's wedding. '

He cursed under his breath. He'd have to drive into town and sort this mess out in person, although another confrontation with Kristie was the last thing he wanted. Especially not when Kristie was sick. Truth be told, he'd probably never be ready for their inevitable next meeting.

'Inform Nurse Donaldson that I'll be there in an hour. It's obvious someone needs to take charge and sort out this mess.'

'Now then, you mind who you're talking to. I've known you all your life. No point adopting your uppity city surgeon's tone with me.'

Alex rolled his eyes but modified his voice to a more respectful tone. 'I'm sorry, Mary. This phone call rattled me a bit.'

'Humph. So I see. Is there anything more I should know then? About you and Kristie?'

'Nothing to know, Mary. Nothing at all.'

He ended the conversation before Mary did what she did best, and pumped him for information. Even if the town had heard that he'd met Kristie in Brisbane, no one had the full story. No one here knew they'd spent many days, and several long nights, together.

No, he wouldn't let his mind go there. Twice bitten and twice shy summed up his love life. Nevertheless, he stared at the phone for a full five minutes as he speculated on Kristie's illness. Was it possible her sickness was more than the flu? Mary had hinted at something else. Did she mean Kristie was pregnant? If so, she couldn't be too far advanced as he'd kissed every inch of her body not so many weeks ago and remembered her gently rounded belly, soft, feminine, and sexy as hell.

He cursed aloud. The chance of any baby being his was a million to one long shot. Long after the fracture in his pelvic bone began to heal, the swelling in his balls had given him grief. Bruising had been so extensive he'd known, long before the surgeons had voiced their concerns, that his sperm count was likely to be either severely lowered, or obliterated. Though, in the back of his mind, he hoped he might one day be lucky enough to father a child. Perhaps after a year or two, when his body had healed, it would be good to do a repeat sperm count and check if things had improved, even a little.

So when he and Christie had finally stopped tiptoeing around each other and fallen into bed, he'd bought condoms, though more for general protection and mutual peace of mind than any thought that he'd impregnate Kristie. A couple of times in their first crazy days together, they'd been so caught up in hot and steamy lust that he'd only remembered at the last moment to pull out a condom.

Yet, between them, they had remembered. Mostly, anyway.

The last night after the wedding they'd slipped up once. Damn! Maybe twice. He couldn't even remember the details because wanting each other had been so fierce, so urgent, so consuming. Nothing like the control he'd needed when Monica had let him make love to her. Her model's body had to be treated like a temple and the slightest bruise or blemish had sent her into a panic.

In contrast, Kristie's nails had cut into his back and left deep crescents and more than once he'd bitten down on her breast or neck. Passionate Kristie hadn't cared. In fact, she'd reveled in his love bites, saying they'd shown how much he wanted her. She'd loved pushing him past the limits of his normal rigid control and turning him into a wild man in bed. And he'd known, in a smugly masculine way, that Kristie hadn't faked her enjoyment when she'd writhed under him, or on top of him. After Monica had left him, he'd wondered if she'd ever been satisfied or if faking orgasms had been one more way she kept him tied to her.

No, no, no! He needed to stop thinking about sex, and especially sex with Kristie. Focus on the knife-sharp pain he'd felt when he'd come across Kristie kissing Mike on that hideous morning. When Monica had left him he'd been angry, with her, and with himself, yet the gut wrenching agony he'd suffered over Kristie's betrayal had burned ten times worse. No, it burned a hundred times.

For the second time, he'd relaxed his guard and let himself believe that a woman wanted him for the man he'd fought so hard to become. Not for his bank balance, his plane, or for his five hundred thousand acres of land. Nor for the elevated social status that went with being either a renowned city surgeon or major share-holder in one of the country's oldest and largest landholdings.

In his disgust, mainly self-disgust, he hadn't waited around for Kristie to feed him any of the same lies that Monica had excelled in telling. He'd left. Turned and walked away as fast and as far as he could. His friends had labelled it cowardly running but his heart knew it was self-preservation. Many times, Kristie had rung, but he'd refused to answer any of her calls. A man could only be made a fool of so many times. Nevertheless, at the thought of a baby, the new life that might be growing inside Kristie, he experienced a flare of hope and a rush of unprecedented joy.

An hour later, Alex drove around the outskirts of his beloved bush town and through the newly-painted iron gates of Dinosaur Valley Hospital. He dreaded the upcoming meeting with his former lover, yet he was driven by a compulsive curiosity about what was happening. Could Kristie possibly be pregnant?

Every time he imagined her carrying another man's baby, his gut cramped. When he pictured her with another man, one capable of impregnating her, he felt let down by his own body. Ashamed that he wasn't man enough to impregnate any woman, most especially Kristie. His stepmother had been almost gleeful when she'd waved the test result under his nose and declared that her children would inherit the family property since a Ryan was incapable of continuing the family line.

Alex swallowed down a rush of bile. If Kristie was pregnant, who was the father? Impotent rage flooded him each time he imagined that the baby might have been fathered by Mike, his mate and husband to his childhood best friend. But he wasn't quite as thick-headed as Kristie accused him of being and his mistrust of his step-mother had grown since he'd come home to Buleroo to recover from his accident.

He'd instigated his own investigation and, hopefully, would have uncovered the truth long before local gossip began speculating about Kristie's close friendship with Mike. The pair had started university together as nurses, but Mike changed from nursing to medicine, eventually becoming the relieving doctor for this remote outback valley.

Mike had met Jenny, his new wife, at the hospital when she'd returned home to help her parents with their sheep station and to become the part time driver for the hospital ambulance. Being the same age as Alex's step-sister, Amanda, Jenny had grown up with them, though despite people trying to link he and Jenny in a romantic fashion many times, Alex had never felt anything for Jenny but brotherly love and best friend closeness.

Within a few weeks, Jenny and Mike had fallen in love and after a whirlwind courtship, had begun planning their wedding. The hospital board had been thrilled when Mike accepted a full time position at the hospital, to commence straight after his honeymoon.

Alex looked skyward for a moment and prayed for strength, before mentally gathering his customary cool armor around him like a cloak. He hooked his sunglasses in one pocket of his shirt and headed for one of the low-slung buildings that made up the hospitals cluster, before striding towards the main office. With the doctor away, Kristie, as relieving manager, would be up to her ears in paper work, apart from juggling the extra workload thanks to being short staffed. Gone were the days when profitable wool exports meant towns literally grew on the sheep's back. Although sheep remained his main money-maker, Alex's father had been forced to expand into several other areas in order to keep the family properties viable. Cattle grazed alongside sheep and several thousand acres were devoted entirely to goats intended for the lucrative middle eastern markets. In the boom days, seven permanent shearing gangs of up thirty to forty men, plus all the extra stockman needed for such large mobs of sheep, had boosted the town's population.

That larger town had supported several full time doctors and a bigger hospital staff but unfortunately, when agricultural profits dwindled, young people looked for work in the cities. Within the shrunken hospital, the nursing director's role had also changed, ranging from hours of boring paper work to standing in as a diagnostic nurse in the doctor's absence.

After tapping on the manager's door, Alex pushed it open and braced himself. 'Kristie, it's Alex.'

A low voice said, 'Come in.'

He nudged the door open and a pair of deep brown eyes, even more beautiful than he remembered, raised to his with an unwavering stare. Even so, the eyes that had haunted him for weeks were now different. They still looked amazing, with irises that had glazed to black when she climaxed. Only now, dark circles ringed her eyes and made their owner look older, sadder. No, don't be drawn in again.

Do whatever is necessary about the missing body and then get the hell out of here.

Alex plunged into conversation, hoping Kristie wouldn't realize that merely looking at her again had shaken him to the core. 'So, you've managed to lose Wilhelm's body.'

Kristie pushed back from the desk and stood, raising herself up to her full height of five feet and three inches, trying to look forceful, despite barely reaching his shoulders. His six feet four inches had often intimidated women, but Kristie had always said she loved that he towered over her as his size made her feel protected. Bloody hell. What was wrong with him? He was doing it again. Letting memories, nice ones at that, take over his rational mind.

'I haven't lost it exactly—'

'Spare me. With your track record—'

'What do you mean my track record?'

'Well hell, in the week we were together—'

'Twelve days.'

'Hmm. I stand corrected. In the twelve days we were together, you dropped your sunglasses over the side of a boat—'

'I wanted to see the dolphins better.'

'You had your camera stolen by a fake tourist—'

'How was I to know he'd run off with it? 'I wanted a photo of us.' Her voice dropped to a whisper. 'Together.'

He tapped one booted foot on the creaking wooden floor as he fought for control. Though he'd cut out his tongue before admitting it, he'd also wanted that photo of them together. Wanted it so badly that he'd lain awake at night and wished he could hold it in his hand and see the way her hair had wound into corkscrews in salt air. Her child-like curls were dark and wispy, all except for that one wild red streak which had been a hairdresser's mistake before the wedding. She'd asked for some little color thing, a touch of daring, but Kristie seemed to attract accidents and her hint of burgundy had translated into a large streak of fire engine red.

His hand lifted from his hip and reached towards the faded red river still noticeable amongst the black, but thankfully he caught himself in time. That hair, and its owner, still looked hot enough to burn. Kristie radiated heat, always had, but he'd ended up as a burnt out shell and, even now, he'd barely recovered. He swallowed. The last thing he needed was Kristie noticing how vulnerable he was to her. How raw he felt being in her presence. He needed her to view him as the chairman of the hospital board and a part time doctor, not her former lover. Yet, for today at least, her stuff ups had become his personal chaos.

'It seems you've landed us in another mess.'

'Us?' She lifted a brow. 'I expected you to tell me it's my mess.'

'I was being politically correct. Too polite to blame you completely. Yet. But we need to find that body before word leaks out.'

She nodded. 'I've sent Joey to Wilhelm's house to speak with his wife and family.'

'You did explain to Joey the need for secrecy.'

Her left eyebrow rose again in a crazy lopsided tilt. 'Contrary to your assumptions, I'm not stupid. I do know what I'm doing.'

He swiveled to the window as he muttered, 'Could've fooled me.'

'What did you say?'

'Nothing important,' he muttered, without turning around.

Luckily, Kristie didn't have a chance to ask him to repeat what he'd said because the emergency line on her desk rang. Snatching up the receiver with one hand, she grabbed her pen and pad in the other and said, 'Kristie Donaldson, Director of Nursing.'

Alex moved back from the window and watched her swing into official nursing mode, showing none of the worry he'd heard in her voice when she'd phoned him earlier. For several minutes she took rapid notes, fired off questions, and murmured acknowledgement. As she wrote, she repeated the instructions back to the Capcom operator in Rockhampton.

'Case number One Four Two. Flying Doctors notified. Ambulance required. Four-wheel drive. Two people for retrieval. Our approximate departure time will be four pm. ETA sixty minutes later.'

Finally finished, she lifted her eyes to meet his and repeated the information in the most efficient way he'd seen at this hospital in many a long day. Dulcie was an excellent Director of Nursing but having held the position for twelve years, she'd adopted a rather more laid back approach to all emergencies.

On an emergency radio line, Kristie sizzled with efficiency and displayed a quick grasp of the situation. Despite knowing she'd worked in Accident and Emergency for many years and hearing Mike sing her praises, Alex had never seen her in action.

Witnessing yet another impressive side to her stirred emotions he'd tried hard to suppress. Who knew that watching a wild haired bundle of energy doing her job could be so exciting? Having it connected to one of his biggest passions in life, medicine, made it even more arousing, and therefore more disturbing. Though he was trying to remember that Kristie was the relieving nurse manager, he couldn't focus on their current situation. Instead, he pictured her in the hotel's king size bed, giving orders. Her orders then had been about changing positions, changing the angle.

'Alex!' She waved a hand in front of his face. 'Earth to Doctor Ryan. There's been a light aircraft crash west of here.'

He blinked, tried to wipe the silly grin from his face and forced himself back into the persona she expected, a dependable hospital board member and detached medical practitioner. Not her previous lover.

'Okay, what do we know?'

'The Flying Docs medical teams have been notified but they can't get to the crash site for at least two hours. Planes from Mt. Isa and Townsville are already out on major retrievals. They'll probably send a plane from Charleville. They want us to go by road and do what we can until they arrive. We may have to transport them here by ambulance, depending on the condition of the victims and on the state of that landing strip.'

'How many people?'

'The pilot and his wife.'

'Okay. Two can fit at a pinch in our large ambulance if they aren't too seriously injured, or we do have the older rescue vehicle.'

'No, we don't. Luke Hatfield, Mike's replacement, was called out to an accident at one of the railway maintenance sites. He took the older ambulance because the new one wasn't ready when he left.'

'I heard the hospital had been hectic for the last week. In fact, I'd been expecting to be called in long before this.' He frowned. 'Why wasn't I called?'

Kristie flushed, glanced away for a moment, before looking back but not quite meeting his gaze. 'Luke's been managing okay.'

Not quite the truth but he'd allow her evasion to slide past, for now. 'Okay, what else?'

'The pilot's wife radioed in to report their position. Her husband is fifty-nine and normally in good health. He started feeling sick and was afraid he'd lose control of the plane, so he tried to put down. Luckily, they were close to an old landing strip on Coondarah Station and he managed to land but the strip is short so he didn't have enough strength left to pull up in time. The plane slid off the end of the runway and hit a tree.'

'Being next to a strip will make it easier for the Flying Docs to land. There isn't a plane at the Longreach Base so they'll send the Pilatus PC Twelve from Charleville. What else do we know?'

'His wife was thrown about a bit. She thinks she's broken a bone in her ankle. Her husband banged his head on landing and is now unconscious, although otherwise unharmed externally. She's trained in first aid so she could report his pulse, color, and pupil reactions. Though she's very worried about why he became unwell in the first place.'

'What do they suspect?'

'It sounds like a heart attack, though it could be an aneurysm. If he doesn't get to surgery, he could die out there.'

'We'd better move then.'

'We?' Her eyes went wide and her jaw went slack. 'No way. You are not coming with me. Jenny's relief ambo is driving for Luke so I'll ring for another driver.'

He cocked one hip, slid a hand into his jeans pocket, and reflected her belligerent attitude back to her. Kept his tone slow and precise. 'Mike and Jenny are both away. Luke is out with our other driver.

That leaves only one person on the call roster authorized to drive the ambulance.'

Kristie's earlier flush of embarrassment had pushed color into her cheeks, but when she worked out who he was referring to, that slight tinge of pink disappeared and she looked pale and even more fragile as she stared at him in horror. 'You.'

Though he was shocked at seeing Kristie here, in his town and his hospital, she appeared even more alarmed at the thought of climbing into an ambulance with him. Why that would be when she had obviously manipulated herself into this job, he had no idea, but he intended using this opportunity to find out. Before she could do any more damage to his life, his reputation, and more importantly, his heart.

He shrugged and feigned a nonchalance he was far from feeling. 'Yes, me.'

'And the nearest doctor, apart from the one standing before me, of course,' she said with a sarcastic roll of her eyes, 'is already out on long distance station visits from the next town. There's no way he can get back here in time to go with me.'

He shrugged again. 'Seems like we're stuck with each other, Nurse Donaldson. I'm the only driver and only doctor, all rolled into one neat package. So, I sincerely hope your emergency rescue skills are up to scratch.'

She hissed in a breath and shot him a look of pure venom. 'Doctor Ryan, our past history doesn't give you the right to criticize my ability. I won this job because of my excellent qualifications. You've obviously forgotten, but when we met, I was working in emergency in one of the busiest hospitals in the city.'

'So why did you leave that position?'

More fire shot from her eyes. 'None of your business. I suggest you do your job and let me get on with mine.'

After a second's hesitation, he dipped his head in agreement but couldn't resist one parting shot, purely to see sparks ignite in those amazing eyes once more. 'I assume the ambulance has been stocked and checked today?'

'Of course it has. I do it myself every morning, according to the orders.'

Her tone dripped ice, yet every look from those unforgettable eyes heated him. What the hell was wrong with him? Concentrate on the fact her earlier vomiting attack could mean she was pregnant, and not the color those eyes changed to when she writhed and climaxed under him. Nor the fact that he longed to see it happen again.

'Okay, we're leaving in ten minutes. Be ready.'

'Doctor Ryan, let's get one thing clear. I'm Nurse Manager and acting in charge here, so you, as a relief driver and relief doctor, will follow my orders. Do I make myself clear.'

Wow! When she was angry, those eyes turned even more beautiful than when darkened with desire. He studied the dusty toes of his boots so she wouldn't see the grin he couldn't suppress. So much for his friends who complained he never smiled anymore. A few minutes in Kristie's company and he was enjoying himself, despite his family thinking he'd never do it again.

No doubt about it. Kristie Donaldson boundless energy and fire had attracted him in the first place and if he hadn't caught her red-handed, kissing Mike, he'd still be sampling that fire. Don't go there, he warned himself for the umpteenth time. Don't get burned again.

'Well, Acting Director of Nursing Kristie Donaldson, get yourself and your equipment into that ambulance in the next ten minutes or—'

'Or what?' For such a little thing, Kristie looked determined and defiant as she peered upwards, a long way upwards, to sneer at him. 'You'll leave without me? I don't think so.'

'Oh, believe me, I will go without you. I'm still the doctor—'

'From what I gather from the hospital staff, you've avoided practicing since your accident. Are your sure your medical skills are up to the task, Doctor Ryan?'

'Touché, Director of Nursing Donaldson. Although I haven't been practicing medicine full time for the last six months, I'm confident my skills are up to scratch. We may be in the outback but I keep up to date with medical journals.' He sighed. 'Fine. We'll forget formality and use each other's Christian names.'

'Ah, but informality between us might suggest that we know each other.' She gave him another knowing smile. 'It was your wish that we appear unacquainted. Remember?'

'Okay, okay.' He threw up his hands. 'For today, I'll call you Kristie and you'll call me Alex.'

Exactly twelve minutes later, ten of which Alex was certain Kristie had spent in the bathroom, they were racing down the town's main street with the blue light spinning and the siren blaring. Glancing across, Alex saw that Kristie's eyes were closed. The black rings around her eyes were more prominent and her complexion had paled even more than before, if that was possible. She looked whiter than a hospital sheet.

He kept his mouth firmly closed although his gaze kept dropping towards her stomach, which was hidden from his view by her navy blue shorts and hospital shirt. Western red dust clung to clothes until colors became indistinguishable so hospital staff wore casual, hard-wearing uniforms.

Kristie's outfit simplified doing laundry and was cost effective but, despite being practical and plain cut, it couldn't completely conceal her curves. Her waist was trim and the slightly-rounded womanly belly that he'd spent a lot of blissful time kissing and licking sat flat under her polo shirt.

Had she realized she might be pregnant? More importantly, would she tell anyone? Because being pregnant would certainly affect her chances of working at the hospital. The fusty old board members were unlikely to award her permanent status if she was a single mother and would be taking maternity leave.

He should be watching for kangaroos on the side of the road rather than watching Kristie sleep and worrying about her future. He didn't have room for any more problems in his life right now, not when his step-mother continually made rash decisions that disturbed the family peace. Though Kristie's appearance in the valley might not have anything to do with him, he couldn't stop imagining what could have been, or imagining what might happen in the future.

His conversation with Mike was long overdue and it was entirely his fault because he'd acted like a teenage boy suffering his first rejection. Instead of confronting the problem like a man and staying around to discuss things the day after the wedding, he'd run away and used the family holdings as his shield against questions regarding medicine, and his love life. He owed it to Mike to not be so arrogantly certain what he'd witnessed meant anything more than a kiss between good friends. Nor so quick to judge and blame his friend, or friends, as he counted Kristie as one of the best friends he'd ever had.

Kristie was harnessed securely into her seat, yet her death grip on the door handle hadn't loosened, even after they'd left the town and were the only vehicle on the road.

'You can relax. Even if you don't see me as a capable doctor anymore, I've driven on these roads all my life.' She glanced down towards his legs. 'My leg is fully healed, if that's what's worrying you.'

She flushed with embarrassment. 'You drove amazingly well in city traffic, but I've never seen you drive an ambulance.'

'Four wheel drive trucks are built for safety. I'll get you there.'

'I trust you.'

He was too stunned to speak. She trusted him, but though he was drawn to her physically, he certainly didn't trust her. Perhaps he'd lost the ability to put himself entirely in someone else's hands when he'd been a boy, and never regained it. He could psychoanalyze himself all day long and never find all the answers.

Every time he'd tried to disprove his father's harsh verdicts about the people Alex mixed with in his younger days, his old man had been proved correct. Time and time again, Alex's judgment had let him down. He'd been forced to accept one of his father's tried and tested rules as his own. When people discovered you were an Undulla Ryan, they invariably wanted to use you in some way. Nobody ever wanted you for yourself.

Kristie's capable hands were clasped over her slim thighs and he could recall how they'd felt on his own thighs, sliding up and down, especially over his naked skin. A shiver ran down his spine at the image of her hands, and eager mouth, exploring his body.

Bloody hell. She was still the most enticing woman he'd ever met. Still sexy, still arousing. Nothing would change that. He swallowed back his thoughts, and wishes, and concentrated on maneuvering the heavy vehicle around the potholes which dotted the road.

'Trouble is,' she said with a sigh, 'you don't trust me. Maybe you'll never be able to give a woman your full trust. Without that, love will die. It always does.'

His hands twitched on the wheel and he wriggled uncomfortably in his seat. She'd read his mind. He could count on one hand the number of women he trusted these days. His half-sister held top spot on his list, alongside Jenny, and a couple of the motherly women from town he'd known his entire life.

His stepmother didn't rate a finger, nor would she ever be on anyone's most trusted list. As for Kristie, he'd crossed her off weeks ago. Or so he tried to tell himself.

3

Kristie slumped down in her seat as far as her seat belt allowed, too tired to continue sparring with Alex. She indulged in a few moments of self-pity by recounting the string of upheavals in her recent life. Her mother's slow death, though physically shattering, had been expected and inevitable. Her brother's long struggle out of the grip of drug addiction, though also physically exhausting for those helping him, had followed some sort of pattern. For weeks at a time, his battle dragged them along an expected path.

Her about-to-be-waged battle with Alex, though stirred by her appearance in his territory, had also been expected and even premeditated. Nevertheless, the strain shattered her. She'd had no time to brace herself for the shock of coming face to face with him, nor to do any of the normal girlie things she'd imagined before she presented herself to him. No new haircut, no pretty dress, no opportunity to present as an ex-girlfriend, rather than a hospital nurse.

And in truth, she'd not even looked her hospital-efficient self, because she'd looked as wrung out as the cook's apron after a hard day's cooking for thirty patients. On top of an epidemic of flu in the town and Wilhelm's missing body, she'd spent the morning hanging over a toilet bowl. Her hand crept to her stomach and she sensed, rather than saw, Alex's sharp stare follow her movements. This morning's upset stomach must be a touch of the town's epidemic virus, nothing more, nothing less.

As they bumped over the rutted road, she gripped the handhold above her head and pushed her head back on the headrest, willing her stomach to settle down. Embarrassing herself by being sick in Alex's holier-than-though presence was not an option. Not when she'd dreamed for weeks of seeing him again, entrancing him with her looks. Huh! What a joke. Her woe-be-gone appearance would send even the strongest man running and Alex would be on the lookout today for any excuse to report her as incompetent. Any opportunity to toss her out of his life the way he had six weeks ago, without listening to an explanation and without believing anyone could be right, apart from him.

She swung one booted foot and kicked at the padded medical pack at her feet. Although the impact jarred, she enjoyed the release of frustration. So she repeated the exercise. Twice more.

'By the look of satisfaction on your face,' he said, and although his voice was quiet against the noise of the diesel motor, she jumped a little in surprise. 'You'd like to plant that boot in something more substantial than a medical pack.'

'Actually, I pictured planting it in *someone*.' She glanced at his groin. 'Right where it would hurt most.'

'Ouch.' He made a performance out of wriggling his rear end into a more comfortable position on the seat. Damn the man. He could still amuse her even while he annoyed her.

They'd grown close when she'd visited Alex, at Mike's bequest, during his recovery after a dreadful ambulance accident, but a string of unforeseen events had interrupted their time together. Then, twelve days before Mike's wedding, Alex, as best man and childhood friend of the bride, had arranged a magical boat cruise for all their friends before the wedding day. Within twenty-four hours, they'd toppled in to bed together with a shared passion more powerful than anything she'd ever imagined.

Days spent exploring the city and nights wrapped around each other had been like a wondrous fairy tale to someone as starved for happiness as she'd been. Dreams of forever had filled her mind, until the morning after the wedding when she and Mike had shared a kiss, a simple gesture of understanding between two friends who'd suffered through the same sibling dramas, and all her plans for a future had blown up in her face as quickly as Alex's temper had flared. In that moment, she'd understood that love had no chance of growing without trust, which brought her thoughts full circle and back to Alex and his ingrained distrust of people.

Four months earlier, Mike had rung her from the outback valley where he'd taken up the position of Medical Officer. He'd begged Kristie to check on an injured and depressed Alex, playing heavily on her soft heart. 'He's in a bad way. Unconscious for three days and now suffering survivor guilt because his ambulance driver mate died at the scene. And his father only passed away a month ago. His fiancé is an international model who's overseas somewhere and doesn't seem to give a damn. He's in your hospital so please, could you visit him. See what he needs.'

'He won't want to see me,' she'd told Mike. 'I'm practically a stranger.'

'You met him at our engagement party and Jenny's worried sick about him.'

Despite her misgivings, Kristie had dropped by Alex's room every day. At first, he'd been withdrawn, difficult, and argued with the staff over his treatment schedules and medication, but she'd owed Mike more than she could ever repay so she'd ignored Alex's sullen attitude and bullied him into cooperating with the hospital staff. She'd dangled information about his beloved valley like a carrot before a stubborn donkey and, by refusing to kowtow to his elite surgeon's status, forced life back into his battered body and numbed brain.

The unfortunate, and unforeseen, twist to their personal situation saw Alex's dependency on her deepen, while his engagement hovered above them like an unburst thundercloud. Alex, go-getting doctor and wealthy cattle baron, was as far out of Kristie's league as the moon was from earth so by unspoken agreement, nothing was acknowledged. After Alex's transportation back to the Valley Hospital for rehabilitation, Kristie had quietly mourned their lost chances and publicly applauded the return of his wayward fiancé. Monica, an international model, had globe-trotted through most of their engagement but had agreed to go to the valley with Alex.

After three weeks of worrying about Alex, Kristie had broken her own rule and asked Mike for news. 'Monica was never going to be right for Alex. When he told her he was serious about honoring his agreement to his father and staying in the valley, Monica dumped him.'

'How did Alex take it?'

'He was devastated. Even having a plane and a pilot at her disposal couldn't convince her to stay in the bush. She thought she was marrying a rich city specialist who'd fly her to the bush occasionally so she could impress her famous friends. Give them a quick glimpse of outback life.'

'Did she expect Alex to follow her back to the city? To leave his family again?'

'Monica was so confident of her own worth she thought he'd beg her forgiveness as soon as he was on his feet again.'

'And that hasn't happened?'

'No. He's staying on Undulla, for a while at least, to sort out the family situation.'

Kristie's new job hadn't reached Alex's ears earlier because he'd disappeared into the widespread bush of the Northern Territory after the post wedding fiasco. Gossip alleged he'd returned two weeks ago, disillusioned and bitter, avoided friends and immersed himself in excessive work mustering cattle. No one knew the identity of the city girl who'd treated their local hero so badly, but people commented that a doctor as nice as Alex didn't deserve to be the victim of such outrageous behavior.

Only Kristie knew she was the girl they hated.

On that ill-fated morning when they'd last seen each other, he'd spun on his heels and stormed out without allowing explanations.

Exactly one minute after he'd chanced upon her in the hotel corridor, outside the bridal suite, soaking the groom's shoulder with her tears and yes, kissing him. Not knowing how much she and Alex had shared, Mike had thought Alex's misunderstanding of the situation a huge joke. Prior to the wedding, Mike and Jenny had been too busy to question the absence of Alex and Kristie and their time together had been too new, too precious, to share.

At seventeen, Alex had left for university to study medicine, despite his father arguing that Alex's place was at home, working the land like generations of Ryan's before him. His father had relented only because Alex had promised to return and practice medicine locally and so continue to be a cattle grazier. When he didn't return immediately, his father had nearly disowned him. Lying in bed together, Alex had confessed to the consuming guilt he'd felt for upsetting his father, who had died before Alex could fulfil his promise. Then Alex's leg had been crushed and he'd suffered internal injuries when a speeding car had sideswiped the ambulance driven by his friend, Barry, as they rushed to an emergency. Barry had been killed instantly.

Kristie had grieved with Alex. She knew his strengths and weaknesses and what made him the man she'd fallen crazily in love with. The man she'd followed halfway across Australia. When she'd seen the call for a relieving manager at the valley hospital, she'd believed fate had offered her a chance to heal their relationship and discover if they could have a future together. Perhaps she could become friends with Alex's twin stepbrother and sister, who he loved so much. From the moment his father had married Eliza and brought her children to live on Undulla, the three had formed a strong bond, clinging to each other through the difficult years of his father's harshness and Eliza's indifference.

Despite the twins being away at university, they remained extremely close, something Monica had seen as another obstacle to deprive her of Alex's time and attention. Because they were not Ryan's by blood, Monica believed they should pay their own way through University but Alex would never desert his family, not even for his fiancé. His compassionate and caring nature was a powerful attraction for Kristie yet Monica had viewed it as a weakness.

After Kristie's mother had died from cancer and she'd nearly exhausted herself time during her brother's long battle with drug addiction, she craved permanency, with a stable home and a loving relationship. She'd come here hoping for another chance with Alex. Hoping it wasn't too late for them.

Alex swung the ambulance over a cattle grid and onto a rough track and headed towards the old air-strip, praying it would be good enough for the Flying Doctor to land safely. If the injured pilot was in a bad way, they'd need to evacuate him by plane to the larger base hospital at Charleville.

'This strip hasn't been used much since the new one was built nearer to the homestead, but landowners out here are always prepared for emergencies, so I'm hoping the strip has been kept reasonably clear,' he told Kristie.

He spotted the plane at the far end of the grass strip and pointed it out to Kristie. 'He did well to land but he mustn't have had enough strength to stop before he hit the tree. It looks like minor damage to the wing. So, it may even be serviceable enough to fly out, instead of having to tow it.'

'I forgot you have your own plane.'

He looked at her with skepticism. 'In my experience, women like you calculate to the last penny how much a man is worth financially.'

'And as I've already pointed out once today, I'm not Monica.' She ignored his angry hiss of indrawn breath. 'I was never interested in you because of who you are, or your worth at the bank.'

'Then why carry on with Mike when you were with me?'

That question had preyed on his mind for weeks, burrowing like a worm into his brain. Nevertheless, he'd never meant to ask. Yet, if he was ever to regain peace of mind, he needed answers. And if Kristie indeed carried a child, he needed to know whose it was. They all did. He didn't want to think how traumatized Jenny would be if Mike's close relationship with Kristie became public, or if anything more was involved. Jenny was his friend, and he wanted her marriage to Mike to be successful.

Accepting the idea of love everlasting was difficult after the damage Monica caused, plus the poor example his father's marriage to Eliza had set for he and his siblings, yet Jenny loved Mike, deeply.

He looked at Kristie, realizing she hadn't answered his question. She stared at him with tears in her eyes. Hell, he was an insensitive idiot.

Their conversation was postponed as he pulled the ambulance up beside the damaged plane and they sprang into action. Medical training took over and the injured passengers became first concern. The pilot was slumped in his seat unmoving, whilst his wife was leaning out of her open door.

After jogging towards the woman, Alex said, 'I'm Doctor Alex Ryan and the nurse getting the equipment is Kristie Donaldson. We're from Dinosaur Valley Hospital and we'll assess you and your husband and report to the Flying Doctor.'

He moved to the pilot's door and eased it opened, careful not to jar the unconscious man. He spoke across him to his wife. 'What's his name? And yours.'

'I'm Grace, and this is Jimmy. Jimmy Lovatt.'

Kristie appeared beside Alex and passed him the emergency kit, which he placed on the floor under Jimmy's legs. She leaned into the open door to wrap a blood pressure cuff around Jimmy's upper arm and read his pressure. Next, she took his pulse, temperature and put the stethoscope onto his chest to check his respiration rate, then reported it to Alex as he checked Jimmy's legs for injury.

The two of them worked in the cramped space as if they'd performed this routine together a hundred times. Alex had never felt so comfortable working alongside a nurse before and assumed it was because they'd shared closer encounters. Every movement was like a well-choreographed ballet. Even focused on his patient, Alex was aware in every pore of his body of the feel and scent of Kristie as she leaned in beside him. Her heat permeated the heavy denim covering his thigh when she pressed closer to Jimmy's side and for long moments, he savored the familiar sensations. If he jerked away, Kristie would recognize the effect she had on him.

With tremendous control, he eased back before his lower body's treacherous response was noted by two keenly observing females. Drawing a steadying breath, he ran his hands over Jimmy's body, pulling up his shirt and checking for any external injury, muttering to himself as he did so.

With a quick smile across to Grace, he explained, 'Sorry, I always talk to myself while I work.' He kept up his dialogue while his hands did a thorough assessment. 'No external signs of injury. No obvious breaks in any bones. But his blood pressure is low, so we have to watch for internal bleeding.'

Alex moved back to give Kristie more room to lift Jimmy's eyelids and shine the torch into each eye. 'Right reacting well to light. Left sluggish but reacting.' She smiled for Grace's benefit. 'And we hear you know first aid and have already done all these checks while you waited for us. Knowing all of that ahead of time was a big help.'

Grace was in obvious pain from the ankle she'd propped awkwardly on the dashboard, using her jacket as a cushion. Yet she still clutched the small penlight torch she'd used to check her husband's pupils before radioing the Bush Emergency Response Service. Bruising and swelling were evident on her foot, but Alex's first priority was to stabilize Jimmy. During the entire examination of her husband Grace remained calm, a real lady, and Alex was reminded of his mother who'd always demonstrated the same sort of strength. A distinct contrast to the contrived helplessness of his step-mother, Eliza. As the lady of Undulla, she expected to be waited on and had never displayed true grit or courage in her life.

'Do you think he's had a heart attack?' Grace's anxious question broke into his thoughts.

'We won't know for certain until we get him into Charleville. They'll do a full medical workup. Blood tests will show if there has been chemical disturbances or changes. But for now, we can check his heart with an ECG and give him some oxygen to help his breathing.' He moved around the front of the plane to Grace's door. 'Can you describe Jimmy's symptoms when he first felt sick?'

While Alex examined her foot, Grace described in detail what had happened. Jimmy had first mentioned mild chest pain but within twenty minutes it had increased, until he was constantly rubbing at the ache in his chest.

'As soon as Jimmy said it felt like an elephant sitting on his chest, I suspected a heart attack,' Grace explained. 'We did the St. John's Ambulance First Aid course together years ago and we keep updated every year with the resuscitation part of it. Living so far out and with all the flying we do, we both like to be prepared for any emergency.'

When Kristie kept Grace involved in conversation, Alex knew she was giving him time to check for other injuries and was also distracting Grace from her increasing worry over her husband. They'd been there for ten minutes and Jimmy hadn't responded. Shock was their greatest enemy at this stage, both for Jimmy if he had internal bleeding, and for Grace as her anxiety increased.

Kristie had covered Jimmy with a space blanket to keep him warm and produced another for Grace. As she spread the lightweight cover, she kept up a conversation with Grace.

'It's great that so many people in the bush have first aid skills. It makes our job a lot easier. So, what else did you notice about Jimmy? Did his color change?'

'Yes, his face changed really fast from reddish to pale and then looked blue around his lips. He said he felt dizzy.'

The older lady looked fondly at her husband and reached out to take his hand again. Grace was battling bravely to keep her emotions under control while her love for her husband flowed across the cabin in gentle waves. Alex looked up and caught Kristie's gaze, knowing what she was thinking.

During the time they'd shared in Brisbane, the emotions between them had been as intense as the look on Grace's face. Neither of them had given it a name, although the word love had hovered in the air between them. Alex was struck by a keen sense of loss.

After his engagement ended, he'd pushed aside all expectation of love-ever-lasting and his parting from Kristie had reinforced his ideas of marriage. Exposing yourself to so much raw emotion always ended in pain. He'd had plenty of time to think about it while he drove the long and lonely roads of the Northern Territory and had decided to never risk his heart breaking again.

Still, looking at Grace's blatant love for her husband made Alex yearn for the same thing, even a tiny part of it. He watched as Kristie worked efficiently beside him. Sure, she was an amazing co-worker in a medical sense, but letting a woman into his life again was risky. But he needed to stop obsessing about his personal problems and do his job. For the next few minutes, they worked in harmonious silence so as not to disturb Grace who had leaned back and closed her eyes, obviously exhausted.

Kristie positioned the portable ECG unit as near to Jimmy as possible and attached leads to his chest with the accustomed ease of a long-term Accident and Emergency nurse. The equipment wasn't as sophisticated as in city hospitals, but for quick diagnosis, it provided ample information and her aim was to get a clear enough readout for Alex to make a temporary diagnosis for her to report to the flying doctors.

A couple of minutes later, she reported the readout. 'He has an arrhythmia and showing some ventricular fibrillation.'

Alex's face was grim with worry as there was a good chance that Jimmy might have a cardiac arrest if they couldn't change his heart rhythm, and quickly. 'Jimmy's heartbeat is irregular which means his heart is contracting prematurely and causing an abnormal beat,' Alex quietly informed Grace.

Kristie wedged the resuscitation equipment in beside Jimmy.

'If that happens,' Alex said, 'we're ready to defibrillate and shock his heart back into normal rhythm. But because there's so little space inside the cabin, it will be easier if we shift you outside to the ambulance stretcher.'

Grace flinched and gripped her husband's hand tighter. 'I need to stay with Jimmy.'

Kristie smiled at Grace. 'We know, Grace, but we need to do

what's best for Jimmy. I'm going to immobilize your foot with a bandage and then I'll help you out.'

'We'll lift you out together, Grace.' Alex's voice brooked no argument.

Kristie frowned as she tried to understand Alex's meaning. Did he see this as a normal medical lift requiring two people, or had Mary said something about her earlier vomiting? Alex hadn't returned any of her numerous phone calls so she had no idea if he still hated her so much that he'd never listen to her explanations. But now wasn't the time to test the waters. Better to do whatever he said and hope for a chance to talk later, when they were alone.

'We'll lift you onto the stretcher, Grace, and you'll be just outside the door so you can see what's going on with Jimmy.'

She wound a figure eight bandage up Grace's leg to keep it firmly splinted and she and Alex, via a fireman's two-person lift, moved Grace onto the stretcher. When Grace was comfortable and warm, they turned back to Jimmy, who'd roused enough to groan.

Alex was speaking quietly and calmly close beside Jimmy. 'I'm Doctor Alex Ryan and the nurse helping me is Kristie Donaldson. We're going to look after you until the Flying Docs can land. They'll probably fly you to hospital once we have you stabilized. Your wife described your original symptoms when she radioed in for help, but can you rate your pain for me from one to ten?'

Gasping for breath, Jimmy whispered, 'Eight.'

'Okay, We'll give you something for that pain as soon as I get this intravenous cannula inserted.'

Kristie slipped under his arm and spread out the tray of equipment he needed to insert an IV cannula into Jimmy's vein, noticing with annoyance that their close proximity didn't appear to trouble Alex as much as it affected her. Determined not to allow her reactions show, she fought to keep her breathing even.

'His veins are a bit flat,' Alex said, half to himself again. 'But that's to be expected from the shock.'

'His blood pressure is dropping,' Kristie announced a few minutes later from her spot tucked under Alex's arm. She released the air from the arm cuff and twisted to look Alex directly in the face. 'His systolic is ninety and his diastolic fifty.' She turned to Grace and asked, 'Is Jimmy on any medication?'

'No, he's usually very healthy. He has regular medical checks for his pilot's license.'

With a few swift movements, Alex inserted the needle, connected the tubing, and started running in a bag of normal saline to keep Jimmy's vein open and to pump in some fluid to bring up his blood pressure. He hooked it onto the plane's door and set the flow meter to a controlled amount. Opening the drug box Kristie had placed beside him, he selected ampoules, first administering Atropine and then Morphine. Holding each with the labels out, he asked Kristie to check the names and doses with him.

Kristie looked at Grace and shrugged. 'Even out here we have to adhere to checks so there's no chance of mistakes.'

They both realized the dangers of leaving themselves open to expensive litigation. Alex might be a multi-millionaire on paper but even graziers were often asset rich and cash poor. And she couldn't afford any more financial setbacks.

Her bank accounts had suffered in the last two years with both her mother and brother's medical expenses. At present, every cent she earned was going towards building her up her nest egg.

Alex snapped the top off the ampoule and drew up the liquid into the syringe, then injected it into the cannula to relieve Jimmy's severe chest pain. His oxygen saturations were only eighty percent so Kristie put a face mask on him, adjusting it to six liters of oxygen per minute.

In a few minutes, his saturation climbed to a healthier ninety- five percent and the bluish tinge around his lips faded. Kristie's relief was mirrored in Alex's eyes as he bent over to read the data.

'Kristie, use the sat phone to radio in. See how far away the plane is and tell them the situation.'

She walked a few steps away from the plane and followed Alex's instructions, relaying the condition of Jimmy and Grace through the central ambulance reporting station.

'The male pilot has a suspected coronary thrombosis but his

condition has been stabilized. He has an IV running and has been administered Morphine. His vitals are improving and his pain level is lessening.'

She went on to give a description of Grace's injuries, and of the condition of the airstrip and the location of the crashed plane.

Alex moved closer to listen with half an ear to Kristie's succinct report. Despite his personal prejudices, he admired they faultless application of her nursing knowledge in an unknown environment. Even with the added duress of his presence, she'd put aside their personal issues and worked steadily and efficiently at his side.

Long experience in a busy city hospital had made her react to any fluctuation in their patients' conditions without a moment's hesitation. The entire time they'd moved around the plane, their movements were in sync. Almost choreographed. A poignant reminder of actions they'd performed in his hotel room's bed a few scant weeks ago.

He tensed his body to combat an almost overpowering longing to know that connection again, to lose himself in another intimate dance with this warm and vital woman. Kristie's magnetic pull was as dangerous to him as the sight of forbidden sweets to a child with diabetes.

One sample would never satisfy, yet anymore could prove lethal. By just existing within his sphere, she made him feel alive, strong, and something he thought never to feel again, needed.

'Alex. Alex, you're doing it again.' Kristie called, jarring him back to reality. 'Earth to Alex. I've radioed in. The plane is twenty minutes out. We need to make sure Jimmy isn't in pain when they take off.'

'Yeah, I know. They can't afford for his pain to worsen in the air.'

They stepped closer to the plane in time to hear Grace's soothing voice reassuring her husband. 'It's all right Jimmy. The plane will be here soon. We'll get you to the hospital and they'll fix you up.'

Grace held her husband's hand, stroking her thumb over it while Jimmy managed to nod to his concerned wife. Alex was transfixed by the love that flowed between the couple. Risking a glance at Kristie, he saw the same expression of awe and yearning. Working together like this was hell for them both.

While Kristie inflated the cuff and checked Jimmy's blood pressure, Alex inspected Grace's ankle. The pressure bandage had restricted further swelling but above the crepe bandage, the swollen folds were turning a nasty purple-blue.

Across the cabin, Kristie reported Jimmy's latest vital signs.

'Pupils now equal and dilating. BP is a hundred and twenty over ninety. General color improved and the cyanoses around his mouth had lessened. I'll turn down the oxygen. Jimmy, can you hear me?'

Jimmy nodded weakly again.

'Good, that's good. The Morphine makes you drowsy but we need to ask you questions, so we know you're conscious. When the plane arrives, We're going to lift you onto a stretcher.'

Alex caught the sound of an engine in the distance. He looked at the strip and shouted, 'Oh, no! Roos.'

Kristie looked up and saw the large group of kangaroos that had arrived to graze on the long grass at the edge of the strip. In dry weather, the best grass pick was where moisture ran off roads, or tarmacs, and roos often moved closer to these areas at dusk. Twenty or more full-grown kangaroos, heads down as they concentrated on eating, were an enormous danger to a plane trying to land. Roos were unpredictable, so they could turn and jump in front of the plane at any time and once one jumped, the others were likely to follow.

Alex ran towards the ambulance, calling over his shoulder, 'Kristie, stay with Jimmy and Grace.' He pointed to the west where the setting sun glowed a brilliant red and where, through the clouds, the dark outline of a plane was visible. 'I need to chase the roos off before the plane comes down on the strip.'

Leaping into the driver's seat, Alex swung the ambulance in an arc and drove dead center down the strip, blasting the horn as he went. The roos raised their heads, sensing danger, and hopped away, though it took Alex three laps of the runway to clear them all. Thankfully, by the time the plane touched down at the end and started it's run towards them, the strip was obstacle free.

Flying doctor pilots were experienced in landing in adverse conditions and knew that every minute counted, so it took only a few minutes before the plane had taxied towards them and come to a halt. Alex introduced Kristie to the pilot and with his helpers, they loaded Jimmy and Grace into the plane. Before take-off, they attached Jimmy to a heart monitor and were all happy to see that his condition seemed to have stabilized.

The whole operation ran like clockwork and the crew on board were impressed. 'Alex, you and Kristie have done a great job getting them ready for transport. Sorry it took us so long.' He nodded to the darkening sky and added, 'We need to get out of here while we still have a little daylight. How about you two?' He looked at them and frowned. 'You both look beat. Are you okay for the drive back, mate?'

Not giving Kristie time to object, Alex answered. 'No way. I was up all night babysitting cows with calving problems. I'm whacked. It's too bloody hard watching for roos in the headlights. And too dangerous.'

Alex glanced at Kristie, who looked shocked and annoyed. She looked even angrier when John asked, 'What about your cute little helper? City girl, is she? Can't handle an off road vehicle in the dark.'

'Probably not. Besides, rain was falling on the road behind us as we drove out here. It'll be far too slippery for even the four wheel drive.'

'Excuse me, gentlemen.' Hands on hips, Kristie glared at them. 'I'm right here, you know. And I can handle an off-road vehicle very well. I've done a defensive driving course.'

Alex looked at the ground, hiding his amusement. Kristie looked outraged at John's assumption that she was only window dressing and of no real use.

John didn't bother hiding his laughter. He held up his hands, palms outwards. 'Sorry, love. Only teasing.' He turned to Alex. 'Whew. You'll have your hands full with this spitfire, mate. And you get to spend the night out here together. Just the two of you. Trade you places?'

When a look of horror spread across Kristie's face, Alex knew he needed to defuse the situation. 'Kristie, ignore him. John teases all the relief nurses. Besides, he's got a gorgeous wife and three kids, all of whom he adores, waiting at home. And John, you're losing daylight.'

John looked at the sky and frowned. 'Damn, you're right. We're off.'

A short time later, Alex stood side by side with Kristie and watched the plane dwindle to a dot in the gloom. He hauled in a deep breath and waited, knowing Kristie wouldn't stay silent for long. He'd known John for enough years to know, though his joking wasn't subtle, he'd meant no disrespect. Still, Kristie's fists had clenched him and she was battling her temper. Sparks were about to fly.

Alex chuckled. Strange as it seemed, part of him looked forward to being berated by her. Part of him wanted her temper and her righteous indignation. Kristie could quite possibly stir his emotions out of their frozen hibernation, where his friends and family had failed. Since he'd been home, he'd flaunted the property like a weapon and used it to keep out invaders. He'd clung to the homestead's remoteness the way a toddler clings to a well-known cuddly blanket, and now that he didn't have his father's continual complaints to deal with, the old house had become his sanctuary.

His father's great grandfather had given his life to developing their vast properties, so a Ryan choosing not to live and work there was inconceivable for his father. During six years of medical school, four years of residency, and working his way up to be a surgeon, his father had only spoken to him on his return visits to Undulla. As a medical practitioner with some knowledge of psychology, he understood his father's constant rejection of him had caused some deep rooted emotional scars. Although understanding didn't stop the pain.

His return to Undulla, though a soothing balm to his battered soul, wasn't enough to heal all his wounds. He felt haunted by memories of his father in every room, and his agony increased twice over when his stepmother reminded Alex that he'd caused his father to die from a broken heart. Rationally, he knew these accusations were unfounded and unjust, but to appease his stepmother, he didn't mention how much he longed to return to his first love, medicine.

Turning abruptly, he strode to the ambulance without looking at Kristie. He wondered how long she'd last before demanding to return to town tonight, probably with her driving the ambulance, though he couldn't let her see how amused he was by her behavior. She'd probably hit him over the head with a stethoscope. Despite his long day and fatigue following the adrenaline rush, he felt deeply satisfied by a day spent practicing emergency medicine again. And a day spent working side by side with Kristie had been a relief after his routine days at Undulla. But this situation, though stimulating, was sure to make him crazy.

Since he'd walked into Kristie's office, his emotions had been on a roller coaster ride and now he was committed to a long night in the back of an ambulance with a woman who could turn him upside down with a smile, or an argument. With more force than necessary, he slammed the stretcher back into its place in the ambulance and prepared the space for sleeping. John had left supplies, so they wouldn't starve.

The trick was to stay busy and keep his mind off Kristie, mentally and physically. Now, if only he could stick to that plan. Inwardly he groaned. What the hell had he been thinking?

The night ahead of him was going to be torture.

4

————————

Kristie realized that a night trapped here with Alex was likely to be fraught with emotion, yet this enforced close-ness might also be her one and only chance to explain. Though, if watching him move around outside the ambulance was arousing her, how would she survive the night inside the vehicle. She hoped they had enough blankets that she wouldn't be tempted to shift close to Alex's warm body as she'd done many times in the past. Until she knew Alex's feelings, she couldn't let him guess how intense her emotions were.

She'd present her defense in a mature fashion and impress him with her sense and strength. That idea lasted less than a minute because the moment he met her eye, she was gone. Nothing had changed and she still wanted him, desperately.

'Sorry.' She realized he'd been speaking to her. 'What do I need to do?'

'There's plenty of wood for a fire. John left tinned food to heat up and we can make tea. How does that sound?'

'It sounds wonderful.'

'The temperature will drop fast when the sun sets, so we need our fire organized by then. It'll give us some light and we can heat the food.'

'Right. I'll collect firewood.'

'Watch out for snakes when you pick up branches, won't you.'

She shuddered. 'Oh, yuck. I forgot the snake problem.'

'Do you want me to do the firewood?'

'No, no, it's fine.'

Keeping her eyes peeled for poisonous snakes, Kristie collected a large pile of wood so Alex could start a warming blaze. He'd placed the stretcher mattress on a blanket beside the ambulance and with the ease of practice, had a snug camp set up in a few minutes. Leaning back against the ambulance, Kristie stretched out on the blanket and thought how lucky she was to be stranded with someone as capable as Alex.

Without thinking, she spoke aloud. 'You're amazing.'

Even in the glow of firelight, she could see his blush. 'I'm only doing what anyone would do.'

'No, only someone with your bush knowledge could be this organized. I'm glad you're here with me.'

He gave her a nod and a quick smile. 'I've been on tenterhooks for the last hour waiting for you to berate me about my decision to spend the night here. I didn't think I'd get away making these decisions for you.'

Watching him heat their food, she leaned back and gave in to the fatigue dragging at her. 'I don't want to fight. I want to sit here and look at the stars and enjoy this beautiful night.'

Alex slid down the wall of the ambulance and joined her on the blanket, being careful to keep enough distance between their bodies. He looked up and pointed. 'See how clear the sky is. How many stars you can see. There's no pollution so everything seems brighter.'

'It's so beautiful.' She sighed. 'You must miss this when you're in the city.'

'Yeah, I do. It's one of the few things that make coming back to Undulla worthwhile.'

She was startled by his frankness. After his accident, he had been so reluctant to speak of anything personal, especially anything concerning his family. 'I assumed there were lots of things you wanted to come back to Undulla for.'

He was silent for a minute. 'I miss some things here but not others.'

She needed to know more before she committed herself to life out here. 'I know you miss your stepbrother and stepsister. What about your stepmother?'

'No, not my stepmother. But I don't want to talk about her.'

'Why not? You live with her.'

'For the moment, I have to.'

'Why for the moment? What happens next for you?'

Alex sighed and closed his eyes. She thought he wasn't going to answer but then he said in a low murmur, his eyes still shut, 'I don't know what the future holds for me, or for the rest of the family. I wish to God I did, because I feel as if I'm just treading water lately, waiting for Ben and Amanda to be old enough to decide what they want.'

'So why is up to you to sort it out for them? Not their mother?'

'Because Eliza wants—' He broke off and dropped his head, running his fingers through his hair in agitation. When he looked up again his hard mask was in place once more. 'Never mind. Those are my problems, not yours.'

She stared at his face, only inches away from hers, and barely resisted the impulse to reach out and smooth over the creases marring his forehead.

'Fine. Guard your family secrets for now. But know this, sooner or later, we'll have to talk about us and what happened. And I'd like you to feel comfortable discussing the real reasons you ran away that day.' She sucked in a breath and spoke through the pain of remembrance. 'And why you refused to let me explain.'

'Huh! I didn't run, and you know why I left.'

'I know the pretext you gave but it was too flimsy an excuse.'

'Perhaps I was too disgusted by your behavior to stay.'

'Or perhaps you were too scared of being thought a fool before your friends again.'

She felt him flinch and jerk his shoulder further away and she felt guilty. After travelling halfway across the country for a second chance with this stubborn man, she wasn't giving him a chance to explain his actions. She put her hand on his thigh and felt his reflexive jump. Hmm. Alex might be as torn by her proximity as she was at having him mere inches away. Perhaps they were suffering the same tumult of emotions. Confusion, hurt, anger, and above all, she was frustrated. Sexually aroused by his nearness and not knowing what to do about it. Feeling daring, she slipped her hand a little higher on his thigh and slid it a couple of inches closer to his groin.

He hissed in a sharp breath and covered her hand with his and held it still. 'What are you doing?'

'Experimenting. Testing something.'

'What? Testing my limits before I crack completely?'

She frowned. 'Alex, what's going on? You're so tense and on edge. Are there problems at Undulla? Is that why you haven't returned to medicine?'

He nudged her hand away and pushed to his feet. 'Why would I tell you my problems? You've come to the outback without explanation.' He stood with his hands on his hips and glared down at her. 'I've learned the hard way that most women aren't trustworthy and past experiences proved that I've no reason at all to trust you.'

'That's unfair. I hoped we might spend our night of isolation having a rational conversation. I'd really like to know your plans for the future. If you intend returning to the city to take up surgery again.'

'Why? What does it matter to you?'

'Since I've been at the hospital, people have said—'

'Said what?'

'Someone started a silly rumor that your accident frightened you so much that you've lost your nerve and can't operate.'

'Who thought up that nonsense?'

She shrugged. 'The hospital staff think it's rubbish, especially after you saved Tim Taylor's hand after his fingers were caught in a crusher.'

He frowned. 'Something's strange. The whole town knew within hours about Tim's operation and yet, another fictitious rumor started about me not operating.'

'Another rumor? What was the first one?'

'Some stupidity about me only hanging around here until my new visiting rooms in Brisbane are finished. Then I'm supposed to be leave for the bright lights without giving a thought to my responsibilities at the hospital here.'

'So, we're back to your future plans but you don't trust me enough to tell me.'

'I'll make you a deal. I'll share my secrets if you share yours. We'll talk about my future.' He glanced down. 'And then yours and your baby.'

Alex walked away, leaving Kristie fuming.

Their meal was a silent affair as neither wanted to shatter their temporary peace while they shared their make-shift dinner. When they finished eating, a decisions had to be made about their sleeping arrangements. In the bush, nights on the wide-open plains could be near freezing and Kristie had no intention of dying of cold when a hot-blooded body was available. Though Alex might think differently.

While he stoked the fire to give plenty of smoke and keep away the droves of buzzing hundreds of mosquitoes, Kristie folded up the narrow ambulance bed and laid the mattresses and blankets on the floor, turning it into one larger bed. The emergency torch had battery power for twenty hours so she fixed it to the wall and turned it to a low setting. When Alex climbed in and looked down at her makeshift bed, she held her breath. Being together in a cocoon of bedding while he still believed she'd cheated on him with his best friend's new husband was probably the last thing he'd imagined when he'd answered her call that morning.

'Good decision,' he said after a long moment and without meeting her eyes.

He dropped down beside her and tugged off his heavy boots and then his belt. She sucked in a deep breath and followed his example, including pulling off the waist pouch that held her scissors and pen.

'All sharp objects removed,' she said with forced gaiety. 'Nothing on me that will dig into your back in the middle of the night.'

He covered his eyes with one arm and threw himself backwards onto the mattress. He gave a long groan before muttering, 'I hope when I wake up in the morning that I can say the same.'

She stared at him blankly for a moment.

'Ooooh, you mean...' She looked at his groin and saw a distinct bulge behind the zipper of his jeans. The faded denim was strained to breaking point.

'Nothing personal,' he said, dropping down his arm and staring at her. 'It's been a while since my friend down there had any action. Think of it as a normal male response to the proximity of a warm female body on a cold night in the bush.'

'I see. Any woman squashed in the back of an ambulance with you would affect you exactly the same way.'

'Yes.' His voice sounded strained and his body was as stiff as a board.

Kristie deliberately stretched out beside his length and wriggled her hips. Her leg was considerably shorter than his so, feeling daring, she tested his reactions. Bending her knee a little, she lifted one foot and ran her toes lightly up the outside of his leg. Alex jumped and his breath hissed but he didn't retreat. Raising her knee, she ran her sock covered toes a further and higher, up and down his leg until she felt his body stiffen.

Barely suppressing her giggles, she purred, stretched, and then curved her body closer to his.

'Hmm, lovely. You're so much warmer than me. It's like being spread out naked on a rug in front of a roaring fire and warming yourself.'

'If you don't stop taunting me, you'll discover my body is hotter than you can handle. And, I'd have you roaring like that fire in a short space of time.'

'Ooh, is that a threat?' She silently prayed that her goading might turn him back into the warm and living male she remembered, and not this controlled and hostile man.

He shook his head and soft black strands of hair floated beside her face as temptingly as anything Satan could offer as an enticement.

'Consider it more of a promise.'

She leaned on one elbow and stared at his achingly familiar face. Stern and harsh in the sunlight when he'd stormed into her office and yet soft in the dim interior lighting. She itched to lay a finger on his mouth and feel his breath against her skin, the way it used to be.

'And what if I want to take you up on that promise?'

'For God's sake, roll over and go to sleep. Leave me in peace.'

She sighed and slumped back onto her small portion of the pillow. Another mistake, as that put her face close to his and his breath touched her skin with gentle warmth. She breathed in the scent of healthy male sweat, fire smoke, and beneath it all Alex's unique smell, and one she'd recognize anywhere. His aroused male aroma called strongly to her wanton female side. If she was correct, Alex lay like a statue beside her and yet he yearned as deeply as she did. Gathering her courage, she prepared to embarrass herself if she'd jumped to the wrong conclusions.

Reaching out a hand, she groped for his fingers. She gave herself no time to second guess what it meant and acted on instinct. She slipped her fingers between his larger ones and held their entwined hands up to the light.

'Look, Alex, we still fit perfectly.'

'Fitting together was never the problem. Staying together was.'

'We could work on that.'

'How?'

He shifted so their noses almost touched and their hands stayed locked together. A small distance was maintained by their squashed arms but Kristie could only wonder why on earth she'd stayed away so long. The reasons no longer seemed strong enough to have given up someone so special but, at the time, her family's health problems had kept her chained to the city, near them, living with them, organizing them, and most importantly, keeping her mother and brother alive.

Her mother was gone now and her brother was doing much better, with the help of a girlfriend who loved him. Alex was no longer attached to another woman. They were two single people who shared a dream to have a happily ever after with a family. For her part, nothing had changed. She wanted Alex Ryan with a longing that awed, excited, yet terrified her. But if didn't take a chance, here and now, she'd regret it for the rest of her life.

Shifting slightly forward, she flicked her tongue over his pursed lips. His breathing caught and he held still, dark eyes locked with hers as she explored his mouth with the tip of her tongue. She licked his lips a second time and sighed into his mouth when he opened a little and she could taste him fully.

'Warm,' she said, not breaking their locked gaze. Her tongue skimmed the inner rim of his mouth and she was gratified when a shudder rippled down his entire length. 'Delicious,' she murmured.

His eyes went wide and he swallowed loudly. She lashed deep inside his mouth with her tongue and he relaxed the muscles around his jaw and invited her to go deeper.

'Mine,' she murmured.

His deep moan rumbled across their joined lips and his hands moved, fast as lightning, as he slid them under her body and pulled her tightly against him. His erection prodded, hard and hot. He pressed, rolled, and rotated his hips until the entire length of him was imprinted on her mind and body. He shifted to lie halfway over her while his busy hands continued to move up and down her sides, roving over every curve with loving attention. Her breasts were crushed under the weight of his chest, but she welcomed it, reveled in the feel of an eager male body covering hers.

She automatically lifted her hips to meet his movements and they rubbed together in a well-rehearsed prelude to sex. Alex's eyes were locked with hers so intensely that she was drawn to him, body and soul. All she could think was that this seemed so familiar, so wonderful, and so desperately needed.

'Alex, please, please. I need you.'

He lifted onto his elbows while she squirmed, a bundle of awakened senses, and hotly aware of each place his hungry gaze touched her as it raced over her features.

'Curse you to hell and back, Kristie, for coming here. Stirring up things I'd tried so hard to forget. Despite everything you did, I still want you.'

'But I didn't—'

He covered her lips with his fingers and shook his head. 'Don't. Don't remind me of the past. I only want now.'

At long last, he dipped to kiss her and their tongues met and tangled in a rush of need. Beads of sweat dripped from his forehead to her cheeks until, with a quick flick of his tongue, he swiped at them before moving back to her mouth. She growled her desperation into his mouth but he didn't stop. Their kisses went on, and on, and on, until want of oxygen made her head spin and her heart hammer against her rib cage.

For what seemed an endless amount of time, they stayed locked in a tight embrace, kissing and fondling. Slipping his hand under her polo shirt, he cupped one swollen breast and she moaned louder. Squatting back onto his haunches, he gripped the hem of her shirt and tugged.

'Lift,' he ordered.

The uniform top flew over her head and caught on a steel equipment rack and she instinctively crossed her arms over her chest. Not because she didn't want his mouth feasting on her aching breasts, but in shame over her tatty bra. Sexy underwear and a tight budget didn't mix. Her secret passion for lacy bras had shriveled in the same way her social life had during the years she'd been the sole bread winner for her family. Doing a quick mental check, she realized with horror that she wore one of her oldest bras, which was fine for a busy working day at a bush hospital and under her dark uniform shirt.

She groaned when she pictured herself through Alex's eyes. While still serviceable, this bra had once been a vibrant hot pink but many washings had faded it to a patchy pink blush. The color of embarrassment heating her cheeks would be ten times brighter than her underwear. And damn it, her panties were the same well-worn color.

Squeezing her eyes shut, she prayed he wouldn't notice, which was, of course, wishful thinking. Alex was very astute, perhaps because surgeons examined women's bodies with razor sharp eyes and infallible instincts. When they'd been together, nothing had slipped past him.

'Where's all your sexy underwear?'

She opened her eyes to see him watching her, his forehead puckered and his hand hovering over her bra.

'This is as sexy as it gets these days.' She lifted her head and peered down, trying to view her disastrous underwear. 'Same bra. Just seen a bit more use.'

His puzzled look stayed. 'Why?'

She managed a small shrug before flopping back on their makeshift bed. 'No money to waste on luxuries.'

'But you earn good money working at your level of nursing. Where's it gone?'

She sighed. 'That's one of those things I can't fully explain. Not yet.'

He sat back, away from her, and she loathed that she'd caused him to withdraw from her again. She shivered. Too many years coping with problems not of her making had worn her down.

Unwelcome tears trickled down her cheeks. 'Oh, God, not again.' She swiped them away with an unsteady hand.

'Kristie.' That one word held a world of anguish.

His concern proved the last straw and her tears sprouted like a broken water pipe. She curled away from him, although his muscled legs still enclosed her. He curled behind her and held her shaking body and the comfort of having him pressed against her back was too much. Her body shook and her wobbly sobs were like those of an over-tired child. He slid his hand up and spread it across her breast in a tender gesture that brought a fresh rush of tears. She sobbed, gulped, and sniffled for a few more minutes while he wrapped around her, a protection against the world, and nuzzled her neck.

When tiny whispers of kisses drifted across her exposed jaw, she rolled to face him and he shifted to cuddle her closer. A few small hiccoughing sobs escaped before her emotional outburst finally ran out of steam.

'I- I th-thought men r-ran away when women cried.'

She felt his chuckle. 'A nice thought, although not always possible. I'm used to comforting patients, and their families, after I've delivered surgical news, good or bad.' He chuckled and a fond smile lit his face. 'Nor is it possible to be Amanda's older brother without learning to cope with numerous bouts of tears. Whenever my father's autocratic rules became too much, I was the one whose shoulder she sobbed on and who had his shirt soaked by her tears.'

'And you love playing the role of big brother.'

He shrugged. 'Having Ben and Amanda to look after when they came to live at Undulla gave me something I'd never had.'

She swiped at her damp cheeks. 'What?'

'Someone to love, and to be loved by. I'd never had that with my father. Oh, I know in his own way he loved me, but after my mother died he decided the best way to bring up a child in the outback was to teach me everyday life was cruel. Only the tough survived and showing weakness was like admitting failure, and a Ryan never fails.'

She touched his face, running a finger over the creases between his brows. 'I'm sorry you didn't have a better life growing up, but it's a credit to you that you're so compassionate now.'

'I had enough. A home and a town I love, which is a lot more than some kids.'

'Material things, but little affection. It's easy to see why you mistrust the idea of loving someone.' When he stiffened, she stroked a hand down his side until he relaxed. 'I only mean that trusting must be hard for you.'

'I've good reasons to mistrust most people's motives, especially women's. But let's forget all that now and you can tell me about your money troubles.'

'Not yet. I need to know you're ready to listen to the whole story. My being short of money is tied up with why I kissed Mike—'

He groaned and blocked his eyes with his hand.

'I'm serious, Alex. When you're ready to listen without any preconceived conceptions, without judging me as another Monica and only after your money—'

'Don't go there!'

'—or as a potential fiancée who didn't stay when you had an accident, or when you stopped being a socially-connected surgeon and came home to work in a country town. When you can see me as a person with problems, but also as someone who didn't wish you harm, then I'll explain.'

'Christ! You really don't play fair. If I don't give you a fair chance, I'll be seen as an unforgiving bastard, but if I forgive anything I saw without knowing why, it could easily come back to bite me. Will you break my bloody heart again?'

She bit her lip. 'No more hurting each other. Please, not tonight. Just kiss me.'

5

A lex's chest tightened at Kristie's plea. He looked from her tear-streaked face to her bottom lip, reddened by her gnawing it during their emotional conversation. To hear such a strong, brave woman beg for his kiss and plead to feel his body spread across hers, soothed his wounded soul.

How could he resist her? She was a sexy enchantress who'd captivated him from the first moment they'd met and thawed his frozen emotions until he'd reluctantly accepted that he was in love. But, as he'd expected, their love had been crushed under the weight of lies and mistrust. Though he accepted that much of the blame belonged with him and his ideas about relationships because he'd never seen many examples of happy ever after couples.

If he wanted a chance at true happiness, he needed to risk his heart again and put himself out there. What did he have to lose? He'd been merely existing of late, not living the life he wanted, as he was caught between doing the right thing for his family or working in medicine. Eliza made it clear that he couldn't have both, not if he wanted Undulla to prosper.

Here though, this moment, he could have another thing he wanted, an important part of his happiness. Kristie, her body, and perhaps even her love could be his if he took those first tottering steps to renewing their relationship and then leave it to fate after this one night ended. So no more thinking and do what she asked and take her. He rolled his hips and rubbed his aching penis across her crutch and, oh my God, she felt good. All he could think of was keeping her with him, trapping her smaller body in an intimate cocoon and never letting her escape.

He tasted her lips and every ounce of bottled up and hidden-away longing surfaced until their kiss deepened and she responded with uninhibited passion. Her mouth was wide and wet and he delved into it, again and again, until she captured his tongue between her teeth and sucked. He bucked and pressed deeper, while cursing their restricting layers of clothes.

She undid his top shirt buttons, pushed it aside, and ran a line of tiny kissed down the cords of his neck. He filled his hand with one magnificently full breast and prodded her harder with his erection until she squirmed, shifted, and widened her legs and all rational thought leached from his brain. Kristie, the sight, scent, and sound of her swamped him.

'Oh God, Kristie,' he moaned, as he slipped his hand under her and released her bra.

Her chuckle vibrated against his chest. 'You haven't lost your touch at undoing my underwear one-handed.'

'I'm shaking so much that it's a wonder I managed it.'

He pulled her bra free and tossed away and palmed a breast, shuddering when it molded as perfectly to his hand as his old fencing gloves. He licked her nipple, reveling in the exquisite taste, and feasted on her, sucking her areola deep into his hungry mouth.

'Yes,' he said, when she arched and offered her other breast. ' I won't forget that one.'

He was distracted for a moment by her fingers tiptoeing down until he hovered on the brink of insanity before she cupped his balls and rubbed him through the denim. With a shaking hand, he reached down, undid his fly, and invited her to do whatever she wanted. Her small palm and spread her fingers investigating his naked flesh made him twitch, aroused beyond bearing.

'Warm there, too,' she murmured, while her fingers worked him. They slid around his penis, moving up and down in the cramped space between his hot belly and the cold fabric.

'Jesus. I can't ever remember getting this hard, this fast.'

With the jerky movements of a teenager, he lifted to his knees and yanked off his pants. When his clothing had been dealt with, he guided her hand to his shaft, knowing his size would show her how urgently he needed her, because he was incapable of anything but praying that she'd hurry. She'd be able to feel the throb and pulse of his veins and know how ready he was, and how desperate to have her. Her grip tightened around him as he thrust between her fingers and he had to bite his lip from screaming out his wants when her bare knuckles rubbed harder on his oversensitive flesh.

'Christ,' he said, as he twisted and wriggled. 'I tried to forget how good it feels when you touch me, but I couldn't. Not when it's never been this good with anyone else.'

His breath caught and hissed when her fingertip grazed his swollen tip and she swept up droplets of his pre-come. With her eyes fixed on his, she lifted her finger to her tongue and, in a slow and mind-shattering motion, she licked. Her tongue swirled before her finger, and his semen, were sucked into her mouth.

'Mmm. Delicious. Salty.'

'You're fucking killing me.' She did it again, slowly and deliberately mimicking their previous erotic dances, until he could swear his chest was about to burst and he was a second away from coming all over her. 'You make me forget everything but how much I want to be inside you. Feel your muscles clench. Know we're both going to –'

He froze. 'Shit! No condom.' The shock was so profound he felt like he'd been dumped into a trough of winter morning water.

Her eyes went as wide as the full moon rising outside. They'd both been too caught up in the moment to consider practicalities.

Stop, pull back, climb off her, his mind screamed. His body, however, refused to obey. Mustering every bit of his lauded surgeon's control, he willed his arousal to subside and commanded his body to relax, but neither obeyed.

'I'm safe,' she murmured from under his heaving chest.

He shook his head. Did she mean she hadn't been with another man, or that she'd been careful? The option he preferred, longed for her to say, meant there'd been no one but him. Like a fool, he wanted her to shout that aloud in their tiny camping space and stop him tormenting himself every time he'd pictured Kristie turning to someone else for comfort.

Unreasonable considering he'd stormed away from the hotel and given her plenty of reasons to hate him and to topple onto another man's lap and seek consolation. Mike had called him everything from an idiot to a coward who was running scarred and too chicken to leave himself vulnerable again. He'd practically goaded her into another man's bed. But even acknowledging that his post-wedding behavior had been stupid and gutless hadn't forced him to swallow his damnable Ryan pride and admit he'd gone off half-cocked. He'd followed one of his father's set in concrete Ryan rules of 'One strike and you're out'.

Horrifying to know he'd reacted exactly as his father would have expected and arrogantly presumed any decision he made by a Ryan, a wealthy and powerful family, would always be correct. His land-owning ancestors had been labelled, squattocracy, which was a derogatory term for outback pioneers who'd acquired acreages by fair means, and foul, and governed them as harshly as British aristocracy used an iron hand to rule the lower classes. Their policy had been to never question your actions in front of the hired help and he'd had those words been drummed into his head through his entire childhood.

Then call him thick-headed, as his father had done on many occasions, because despite his vow to remain aloof from Kristie and her love life, that arrogant voice in his head beat out the same refrain of prove you didn't cheat on me, show me you can be trusted, and convince me I'm not a gullible fool. Because he'd also been taught to expect that others would apologize to him first, so a Ryan never admitted mistakes if they could get away with it.

During their time together, a chance meeting with Kristie's long-past boyfriend had skewered Alex with never-before-experienced jealousy, which was a ludicrous state of affairs for a man of his age and experience. And ridiculous in an age when girls were allowed do as men had been allowed throughout history and have sex with multiple partners.

'And I haven't...haven't...' So much for being a cool medical professional during this conversation. He could barely speak. 'I haven't been with anyone. Since you, I mean.'

He reluctantly shifted to one side to remove himself, even marginally, from the temptation of fucking her until she screamed out his name, over and over, and to hell with any consequences. Forcing himself to talk about his normally taboo subject was difficult, but he needed to clear the air.

'The chances of me producing enough sperm to impregnate any female are...Probably a billion to one.'

She snorted, an unmistakable noise of disbelief. 'You said that as if you're reciting straight from a medical journal and not talking about something so important.' She touched his face, connecting them, and conveying unspoken sympathy. 'And as I've said before, I think you're wrong because the testing done straight after your accident when your testicles looked like oranges is most likely to be inaccurate. Besides which, believing you're sterile without positive proof is incredibly naïve, especially for a doctor.'

Her words reminded Alex of his most recent argument with his stepmother after he'd been hunting the office for his medical records and Eliza had become defensive. She'd accused him of not trusting her judgment while he'd been hospitalized and of criticizing the way she'd managed Undulla before he'd returned home. Her answer had been to search the hospital files here if he wanted to know more about his treatment but, in one of her lightning-fast mood swings, she'd sympathized with him for losing his mate in the accident.

His father had kept a tight leash on his wilful second wife and Alex knew better than to let Eliza scent weakness, yet her overdone pity over his inability to father an Undulla heir had embarrassed and unmanned him. Her children were prime examples of Eliza's ability to find someone's weakness and prey on it until the victim yielded to her will.

His low sperm count had become a forbidden topic and he hadn't placed a request with the hospital clerk to retrieve his old files from the city archives. Was he being circumspect in dealing with one of his few remaining family members, or fearful of finding a truth he couldn't accept?

'It's...it's what I was told.'

Contrary as ever, Kristie giggled. Her laughter vibrated against his body like the rocking motions of a pay-by-the-coin massage bed and his sex-starved body came alive again.

'Don't you see, Alex? It's ironic, and hilarious actually.'

'I can't see anything funny in our situation.'

'Think about it.' She poked a finger at his chest. 'If you're right and you're sterile, having sex won't matter because I can't get pregnant. And if I'm right and you're capable of fathering a baby, we should've taken more care about using condoms before because it might already be too late.'

Her eyes went wide and she rubbed her stomach in gentle circles. 'Could it be true?'

What could he possibly answer? Yes, I think you're probably pregnant but no, the baby can't possibly be mine. Far better to stay silent.

She rolled her bottom lip between her teeth, back and forth, reddening it again. Before he could stop himself, he swept his tongue across the stressed area and lathed it in moisture, soothing it and her. And as a consequence, exciting himself.

'Nevertheless,' he said, his voice a hoarse growl. 'Having unprotected sex now, when you could be pregnant, is a really bad idea.'

She stilled and dropped her gaze but when she looked at him again, her longing was evident. 'We're both safe. And I want you.'

He hauled in a long breath and berated himself for only thinking like a horny male and not a doctor. If he had sex with Kristie now, he'd be admitting he trusted her word. Although she'd been astounded by the possibility of being pregnant, she truly believed that if a child grew in the soft belly squashed beneath his harder one, he'd fathered it. Apart from that, he'd be putting his faith in her declaration she was safe and accepting whatever that entailed.

However, if he moved away from her now, he'd regret it for the rest of his life. There was no decision to make because wanting Kristie outweighed every sensible consideration. He concentrated on removing the remainder of her clothing.

'They match,' he whispered. 'Faded pink is now my favourite color.' Her panties almost tore in his rush and his breath came sharp and fast as he exposed each hidden inch. He brushed his fingers through her curls. 'I've changed my mind about the color. I'd forgotten how much I love red, sweet and soft red.'

He left one hand tangled in her curls as he dipped to kiss first her mouth, then her nipples. A light brush across her lips followed by a deep pull on a pouting nipple and letting the bud slide between his teeth at release. Her back arched up and she thrust her breasts towards his mouth, a silent plea. Taut nipples enticed, while her breasts fuller curves and swells fascinated him. Obeying her demands proved no hardship at all.

After running his hand around her waist he hesitated, fleetingly, before he spread his palm over her womb and she shivered. A tiny upward curve hinted at a new life that could be growing there. Could he have helped create that life? An unfounded notion and wishful thinking from a man who'd give his right arm to be a father and who'd forgo city surgery in the blink of an eye for the chance to raise a son or daughter on his properties. A vision struck him of the possible fetus under his spread fingers growing to adulthood and following in his footsteps, becoming an experimental surgeon doing good for mankind instead of a self-centered and grasping Ryan.

The idea made him yearn to claim this woman, a possible mother no matter whose baby she carried, for his own. To claim Kristie and keep her. But for now, he'd be happy satisfying them both through the rest of the night.

Suddenly, the hours until daylight seemed far too short.

6

———————

Alex kicked a stick further into the fire with the toe of his boot and prepared to break the silence. This waiting game, played since he'd woken Kristie at dawn with a cup of tea, rattled his nerves. Last night had slain him as it had been one of the best nights of his life. They'd made love in the back of an ambulance for God's sake, and not just once, but three incredible times.

All he could think this morning was, Wow! Yet glancing at Kristie for the tenth time in five minutes, he knew she wasn't as jubilant as him this morning. Something appeared to be wrong, very wrong, and in all modesty, he didn't think it was the sex.

Hell no, because her out-of-control passion had nearly blown his mind, and it had sure blown his body. Muscles he'd not used recently for that sort of work out ached, though in a good way, and she'd been with him every step of the way. She'd bucked, screamed, and reached so many peaks that he'd worried she might pass out. Surely multiple releases rated pretty high up the scale. So why was she dragging herself around as if she'd been hung out to dry wet. If he didn't remove a few bricks from her fast-growing brick wall, they'd be back at the hospital and he wouldn't have a clue what was troubling her.

'They say emergency nurses become addicted to the adrenaline rush.' Tossing that opening into the chasm between them, he prayed that good manners, if nothing else, would prod an answer. 'Is that why you work in emergency?' A sarcastic rebuttal or even her yelling at him would be better than this tense silence.

After a moment, she threw back her head and laughed. 'Yeah, right. On a busy weekend, you don't even get time to get addicted to a cup of tea. Aching feet, no meal breaks, and drunks throwing up on your shoes.'

He heaved a long sigh of relief. Nothing had changed if they could still challenge each other and debate arguments with as much passion as they made love.

'Then why do you do it?' His question was mainly to keep her talking, although he truly wanted to know why she'd quit a job she loved to go bush. As soon as he asked the question, he regretted it because his intention wasn't to provoke a fight. He preferred seeing Kristie peaceful, relaxed, and his, even temporarily.

She shrugged. 'I like helping people in trouble. Even our regulars, the frequent flyers, come looking for help. Someone to talk to and dress their cuts. Feed them tea and sandwiches. I love the fast pace and working on a dozen problems at once because, at the end of your shift, you've stopped people's pain, and maybe saved someone's life.'

He took her hand and squeezed her fingers. 'I'm the one in pain this morning. Put me out of my misery and tell me what's wrong. An hour ago, we were rolling around and getting hot and sweaty and now I'm barely getting two words from you. Are you regretting what happened?'

'No, last night was wonderful. Perfect. Even better than before.'

'What then?'

She pulled away and paced towards the small fire he'd stirred to make tea. 'It's–it's too perfect. Something always goes wrong.' She snorted, a sound of self-derision. 'Trouble follows me. Maybe I shouldn't have come here.'

'No. I admire your courage in making the first move.' He shrugged. 'Perhaps it's the way I was brought up.' He swallowed hard but forced himself to continue. 'I'm mistrustful of everyone and everything, but that is still no excuse for leaving you without having the good manners to say goodbye. For that I apologize.'

'But what if it turns out I'm pregnant? Will you be pleased that I'm in your valley? Will you want me to stay?'

He turned to watch the sun's struggle to rise above the tree line. Nature was far easier to understand than human entanglements. 'If you are pregnant, the baby is unlikely to be mine. In that case,' he said, knowing his voice was as stiff as his stance but unable to relax either of them, 'the baby's father will be involved in both your lives. My being around would only complicate things.'

She stepped around him, stood chest to chest, and glared at him. 'Why do you insist on making things more difficult than they need be? I agree that a baby will complicate our relationship, but I'd expect you to be involved more than anyone else.' She poked his chest again. 'Because there's only been you, for a long, long time. Only you.'

To his dismay, no consoling words ran glibly off his tongue and, despite knowing he was quoting results from a sperm test he'd never actually sighted, he couldn't summon a single word of comfort. Nothing to stop Kristie concluding he was a snake, the lowest of the low, who'd disappeared once at the first sign of trouble and in all probability was about to do it again. The silence lengthened and tension shimmered between them, hot and red like the sun's rays. He was relieved when it was time to start the drive back to town.

Twenty minutes later, and for the third time during their drive back to town, Alex pushed hard on the brakes and brought the ambulance to a dead stop in the middle of the dirt road. 'Pull over,' she'd yell, moments before both hands came up to cover her mouth. Luckily, on this deserted country road the chances of another vehicle appearing were slim.

This time, Kristie had pushed the door open but hadn't climbed down from the high vehicle before what remained of her breakfast muesli bar and tea had rushed up. By the time he reached her side of the ambulance, she'd slid out of the door, dropped to the ground, and sat propped against the side. Thick red dust from the ambulance smeared her clothing, yet she clung to the vehicle as though it was her lifeline.

Not saying a word, he handed her a water bottle and cloth. With a grateful nod, she accepted his offerings, rinsed her mouth and washed her face. He was thankful when a little color crept back into her blanched cheeks.

To give her privacy, he moved away a few paces and stood, feet spread wide, on the dirt road. He kicked idly at a stone, his hands hooked in the pockets of his faded jeans, and totally at ease within this setting. As a boy, he'd learned from aboriginal stockman to wait with patience for things to happen in this unforgiving land. Seasons changed, rain came, cattle prices rose and fell, and stockmen endured. Here, the immaculate city doctor could disappear and only had to reappear when he was forced to don the mantle his step-mother preferred, that of a wealthy outback grazier.

While he waited for Kristie to recover from her third bout of sickness, he tried to practice the same patience, despite knowing the same thought had been racing through both their minds for the last sixty kilometers.

He waited until she'd recovered enough to stand upright and swallow more water before he made his announcement and watched it drop like a lead balloon between them.

'You really are pregnant.'

7

_____

For the life of her, Kristie couldn't work out why Alex sounded so sad and resigned. For her, being pregnant would be a miracle, despite her rational min screaming 'No, no, no.'

When Alex had explained a little about his low sperm count in Brisbane, he'd been a true gentleman and forewarned before their relationship developed further and giving her a chance to walk away. His revelation hadn't simply been, as some men would let it be, an excuse to not use condoms.

Their relationship developed so fast, and with such intensity, he'd been afraid the news would devastate her if he announced it later so he'd laid out the stark, daunting, and devastating facts. Devastating for her if she became further involved with him, but mainly an unthinkable situation for a man who longed for a family of his own.

Like most girls, Kristie had imagined her wedding, followed by two point five children and a cozy house with a back yard to mow. Meeting Alex had brought out her nesting instincts so his news was like sticking a pin in her bubble of dreams. In a fit of bitter disappointment, she'd vowed to treat their time together as a fling. They'd enjoy a few weeks of mind-blowing sex and then say goodbye.

It had taken only a few days to she realize she wanted more than a fling and so did Alex. They'd tiptoed around the subject of adoption and the sad plight of orphans in undeveloped countries, and adoption had seemed a solution. Now there was a chance she might be carrying the baby she'd always dreamed about, and it would be Alex's baby. Instinctively she touched her belly, where a tiny miracle might be growing and, for the first time that morning, she smiled.

'You'll have to tell Mike straight away. He deserves to know first.'

Too sick, and too caught up in her fantasy, to comprehend his meaning, she shook her head. 'What does my possible pregnancy have to do with Mike?'

'Every father has a right to know.' Before she could recover enough to answer, a look of horror broke over his face. 'Unless it really isn't Mike's.' He swallowed deeply. 'Which means you slept with someone else.' His tone was raw, angry, but mainly accusing.

When another wave of nausea hit, she was way past her being-nice. 'Of course it's another man's baby, you dense idiot.' This was like being trapped in a second rate movie, one where the baby's father denies all knowledge of the mother until twenty years later when he's dying and he begs forgiveness from the child he'd wronged. She would never allow a child of hers to suffer such unnecessary grief, especially not after the lifetime of hurt she and her brother had suffered from not knowing their father. She'd fight tooth and nail to give her baby the things she'd been denied, a willing father, a happy home, and being loved and cared for.

Alex was correct about one thing. Every man did have a right to know if he was going to be a father and she'd not deny him, especially when she knew he longed to be part of a family. They were within arm's reach of their own happy-ever-after ending, even if he was too weighed down by his miserable past to recognize it, but luckily for Alex, she was a fighter.

'How can you be such a stubborn bastard? If by some miracle I'm pregnant, only one man is responsible.' Hands on hips, she faced him. 'You!'

His jaw dropped. Alex was unused to people, especially nurses, challenging his reasoning and he was understandably shocked, but a flicker of emotion, perhaps hope, crossed his face. A small lifeline to cling to, encouragement to believe their lives may evolve how she pictured them and, to be fair, discovering you might be a father after being told there was little chance of it happening would stun any man.

None of this would be easy for Alex. He'd be weighing up, as a doctor, whether to accept the medical evidence or to believe her. Clearly he craved children, but his training had taught him to be logical, scientific, and to dismiss unreasonable ideas whereas her actions and reactions at present were based purely on emotion.

'Those last few days in Brisbane when we didn't use protection, I thought you understood. The condoms I bought were never because of the chance of pregnancy.'

'Obviously, there was a chance, though admittedly a small one. But that slim chance must have happened.'

He was walking in small circles and running his hands through his dusty hair. Turning to face her, he scowled. 'I was being socially correct. We stopped using protection because neither of us had been with anyone else since we'd had medicals.'

His stumbling explanation made her want to put her arms around him and comfort him. Although by clinging to his far-fetched idea of either Mike or some other man being the father of her baby, he'd condemned her for a second time. Resentment over his arrogant assumptions revived her fighting spirit.

'Arrogant bloody-minded surgeon,' she muttered.

'What did you say?'

She stepped away from the ambulance and, despite legs like soggy noodles, stiffened her spine.

'You're acting like one of those God's-gift-to-the-universe surgeons, the ones nurses hate.'

'Rubbish. I never act like I'm God's gift to anyone.'

She faced him, hands on her hips and brows lowered. 'You. Are. Now.'

Poor man looked about to swallow his tongue and his obvious discomfort deflated her anger.

'Testing isn't infallible, Alex, and you were too sick to know what was going on for a lot of the time.'

'You expect me to simply believe my results were wrong?'

'I understand your skepticism. Given your unusual circumstances...'

'There's nothing unusual about women lying and cheating. In my experience, some women will do anything, even become pregnant, to force a man to support them.'

She flinched. Though Alex could definitely be pig-headed, she'd never known him to be deliberately cruel before. 'I'm not after your money and I never was.'

'But you must have slept with at least one other man, and in a short space of time. At least be honest and tell me why you did it.'

'I told you the truth. I'd only been with one man in my life before you. Gerald broke off our engagement when my family needed my help. He expected me to be at his beck and call and he hated that I gave my time to helping my family.'

'You've forgotten. I saw you kissing Mike the morning after his wedding. And don't bother lying and telling me Jenny was there too, because I checked.'

'You checked?'

'Yes, more fool me but I went back after I saw you leave Mike's room. Told myself I'd jumped to conclusions and that there must be a rational explanation for what I'd seen. I prayed that Jenny would open the door because I'd have known that you were within sight of his bride when you kissed Mike.'

Kristie frowned as she tried to remember. 'Jenny had gone to her parent's room to say goodbye.'

'So I discovered. You must have scurried down to the bridal suite to indulge in a long farewell kiss the moment Jenny left.'

'I was thanking Mike for his friendship over the years.'

'Ah, yes. Back to the mystery of why you and Mike are such close friends. If you won't explain, why should I believe you?'

Though his sarcasm rankled, she tried to stay calm and be reasonable, knowing that his world had been rocked even more than hers in the past day. Unfortunately, she, Mike, and their two brothers had made an unbreakable pact.

'I can't tell you until Mike gets back. Those secrets aren't mine alone, or even Mike's, and other people might be put in danger if we talk about too soon.'

'So, what do you want me to do? Work with you as if nothing has happened? Pretend you aren't pregnant.'

'I'm asking you keep an open mind, and at least do another sperm count.'

'And what if I refuse? How are you going to get my money?'

Even to her own ears, her bubble of laughter sounded a little hysterical. 'There's always a paternity test later if I really wanted to rob you blind.' She touched her stomach. 'Besides, this whole argument is probably irrelevant because I'm not even sure.'

He glanced at her waist. 'I'm sure.'

'How can you know?'

He snorted. 'You're forgetting last night. I remember what your body felt like two months ago and it's different now. More rounded.'

His gaze dropped to her chest and her sensible hospital shirt felt transparent because her nipples, easily aroused, pushed at the fabric until she crossed her arms over her chest in a childishly defensive manner. The man aggravated and unnerved her even while he excited her.

'Believe me, I had no idea I might be pregnant when I took the job at the hospital.'

'Then why did you come to the valley?'

'Are we back to that again?'

'Until you give me an answer, that question will hang between us.'

Unable to stand up without swaying, she slumped down to the running board. 'If I tell you I came because I missed you, will you believe me?'

His face, with pain etching deep lines of worry between his brows, screamed that this proud man wanted to believe her but he'd had no role models and no family formula to allow him to trust women.

'Kristie.' It sounded like an accused man's plea for leniency. 'I don't know what to think. What to believe.' He straightened to his full height and stared down at her. 'If you want to prove who the father is,' he said, back to his detached clinical tone, 'you'll agree to a paternity test.'

The enormity of what he implied angered her. 'You've the cheek to call me a liar when you won't consider you may be wrong about your sperm count. You're asking me to take a risky test to prove that I'm telling the truth.' She hauled herself up. 'No thank you, doctor high-and-mighty Ryan. A man who can't trust my word isn't the sort of man I want to be involved with, or to have in my baby's life.'

Standing up took an enormous effort and she swayed dizzily but stubbornly waved away his unspoken offer of assistance. Her emotions were too raw to deal with his hands on her now.

In strained silence, they climbed into the ambulance and, with twice as much power as necessary, Alex gunned the engine and sped down the old runway to the grid. When they hit the dirt-road, Kristie grabbed the head-height safety handle with one hand and her stomach with the other. Alex sucked in an audible breath, muttered her an apology, and eased off the accelerator. From then on, he watched her like a mother hen with its chick, which made her more determined to hide her escalating nausea. She closed her eyes and prayed for either her stomach to stop churning or to reach town before she disgraced herself again.

Against all odds, she'd clung to the faint hope that he cared about her, and about them. It was time to give up on her dream and face reality. Time to let go.

He drove for another ten minutes before saying, 'My stepmother is convinced that I'm incapable of being a real man and fathering a child.' He gave a dry laugh. 'In fact, she's taunted me with the results of my tests ever since I came back.'

She waited, eyes closed, hoping he'd explain more about the demons haunting him.

'Eliza believes Ben should be given Undulla when he finishes his Agricultural Degree because, of course, my father had no idea there'd be no more Ryans to inherit our land. And though Ben's children won't be Ryans by blood, Undulla will at least stay in the extended family. Legacy meant everything to my father and as Eliza often tells me, often, it's one more way I let my father down.'

Kristie couldn't imagine why a man like Alex tolerated Eliza's interference. 'Has Eliza also decided what you should do after you oh-so-nobly sign over your inheritance to her son?'

His fists clenched on the steering wheel. 'She wants me to stay here, in an advisory capacity, and to help Ben adjust.'

She sat up straighter. 'Ridiculous. If Ben wants to come back, you'll be free to return to what you love most, surgery.' When he didn't contradict her, she tried again. 'Why are you letting Eliza manipulate you? It's as if she's publicly declared you only half a man because you don't have a son to inherit, and that simply isn't the truth.'

'Isn't it? What woman wants a man who's sterile?'

'You're forgetting that I moved here, to the outback, so I could understand why you love it so much. Don't you get it, Alex? I wanted to learn more about you. Despite knowing about your low sperm count, I came because I couldn't help myself.'

She laid her head back and closed her eyes, but before she gave in to the overwhelming fatigue she said, 'Because, Doctor Ryan, you're more of a man than anyone I've ever met.'

8

For several minutes, Alex sat in stunned silence. By the time he'd recovered his voice, and his equilibrium, Kristie had slumped deeper into her seat and fallen asleep which, ironically, left him nothing to do but watch over her like a mother with a newborn. Though he had no direct link to her baby, his medical instincts insisted he do everything possible to protect a precious new life.

He drove carefully, dodging potholes, and mulled over the past twenty-four hours. Kristie's arrival, and her unexpected news, had disorientated him. Uncertainty and self-doubt weren't normal for him and it didn't take a psychology degree to understand why discovering his ex-fiancée was a money grasping bitch had deepened his mistrust of women's motives.

He glanced across at his troublesome companion and cursed under his breath. For a short time last night, he'd viewed the future, possibly with her, through rose colored glasses but in the hard light of day, he needed to accept that for him there'd be no baby and probably no loving wife. If only he could content himself being a doting uncle to any nieces and nephews and not yearn for the impossible.

Bang! The noise from the blown tire echoed like a gun blast

through the bush. After a hard struggle with the steering wheel, he brought the ambulance to a skidding halt amid a shower of dust and gravel. His held breath whooshed out.

When Kristie jerked awake, he reached across to touch her arm. 'Are you all right?' His hand moved towards her stomach but he stopped himself in time.

'What happened?'

'A tire blew. Won't take long to change.'

'Do you need my help?' She pushed herself into a sitting position and covered her stomach the way he'd seen countless women do during their pregnancies.

'No, sit here out of the dust and rest.' She looked edgy, ill, and she'd had an exhausting twenty-four hours. 'The pneumatic jack makes the whole thing easy.'

He'd changed tires on these roads before he was old enough to hold a driver's license, thanks to his father's beliefs on total self-sufficiency, and although these tires were much heavier than the average, it didn't take him long. Squatting beside the fourth tire, he was tightening the final wheel nut when a shadow wavered between his feet.

Christ, a fast-moving snake. Before he could retreat, the snake uncurled its sleek head, lashed out, and pierced his forearm, before recoiling and slithering away under the truck. Snakebite first aid had also been hammered into him from childhood, so as each ingrained instruction ran through his head, he began the procedure.

Remain as still as possible.

Stop the flow of the venom to his heart.

Above all, stay calm.

He slid to the ground and raised his arm in the air. Using his teeth and other hand, he wrapped the cleaning rag around his forearm and tugged.

Turning towards the passenger's seat, he hissed. Psst! Hey! It took three tries before his calls attracted Kristie's attention and by then his leg was swollen and throbbing and he was barely beating back unconsciousness. At last, she'd glanced in the side view mirror. Her piercing scream jolted him back to consciousness.

'Alex! Oh, no, no! Please, God, no.'

Kristie saw the cloth and realized that Alex had attempted to stop venom flowing from a bite. She dropped to her knees in the dust beside him. 'Don't move. Did you see it? What was it?'

Barely moving his lips, he murmured, 'Brown. King Brown.'

The words sent dread racing through her mind while her blood ran cold in her veins. King Brown, one of the world's deadliest snakes. Any bite meant rapid deterioration and possible death. To stay alive, Alex couldn't even twitch. Not until she immobilized the bitten limb and injected him with anti-venom. Forcing an outward show of composure, she met his eyes and matched her tone to his, soft, calm, and controlled.

'You. Will. Not. Die. I won't let you.'

His eyelashes drifted down until he watched her through tiny slits and his body lay splayed in the dust as still as a corpse. He said each word as a separate, slow whisper. 'Venom. One hundred. Fifty milligrams. One strike.'

'Stop talking! I know.'

She pressed her fingertips onto the vein on the inside of his wrist, registering the erratic beat of his pulse, and watched the slow rise and fall of his chest to count his respirations. Taking observations, luckily, was as automatic to nurses as breathing, because if she dwelt for even a second on whose life was in danger, her medical checks would grind to a standstill.

'Most,' she said, swallowing rapidly to calm herself. 'Snake victims survive.'

His eyes widened. 'Not ... browns.'

She shook her head, trying to block out his words. If she listened, she'd surrender to the waves of panic rising up in her gut.

'Don't move. I'll get antivenom.'

'None...' His eyes held the knowledge of imminent death. 'Here.'

'Luckily for you, there is today.' She willed him to take notice, to understand, to not lose hope. 'After three snake attacks last week, we added antivenom.'

She wrenched open the back doors, gathered the equipment she needed in her shaking arms and stumbled back to where Alex lay as motionless as death. Her chest seized mid-breath but, clenching her teeth, she carefully placed the vital antivenom on the ground before she gave in to her raw fear.

She lifted a trembling finger and held it under his nose, praying silently, until she felt warm air brush her finger. She squeezed her eyes to stop any involuntary tears leaking and dropped her head towards her chest, allowing herself one fleeting moment of sagging relief before she regained control.

Alex mustn't guess how close she was to losing it. She needed to hold it together, for his sake, and for both their sakes. Slipping out of her role of frantic lover and back into her role of nurse, she removed his makeshift covering and placed a wadded bandage over the two red pinpricks where the fangs had pierced. Beginning at his fingers, she crisscrossed the bandage up his arm, tightening as she climbed. When she'd finished the first bandage, she started another and kept overlapping until she'd encased his arm from fingertips to armpit, in bulky mummified white.

The entire time she worked, she recited the first-aid procedures for snake bite aloud. Partly to let Alex visualize each movement without having to open his eyes. Partly to break the deafening silence.

First priority. Pressure immobilization. She slipped his arm into a neck sling, pointing the arm skywards, and leaving his fingertips exposed to do regular checks on his skin color and circulation. Using her teeth, she ripped open the plastic around a cannula and readied IV tubing attached to a bag of diluted Saline solution. She injected the antivenom into the bag and laid in on the ground beside her. His unnatural stillness terrified her. Either he didn't dare move for fear of pumping venom further through his body, or he'd slipped out of consciousness. There was no time to look. Talking to herself as he'd done at the plane, she repeated verbatim her recently learned rural competency course.

For brown snake envenomation: administer two ampoules of antivenom through IV. Very slow rate.

She prayed Alex had identified the variety of snake correctly, as the coloring of Browns varied enormously, but using a snake-specific antivenom, such as this one, would give much better results than a generalized one. Her only other alternative was to swab the site and wait until they reached town, when the hospital could do more specific venom tests.

She glanced at Alex. Chances were slim of him surviving until the hospital and time was running out. Yet even while the clock in her mind ticked off the dwindling minutes, she hesitated, frozen with fear. Her hand hovered above his vein, the tightly gripped needle digging into her skin. Alex's brow dripped cold sweat and hers now matched it, droplets falling from her brow to splash in the dust beside them. To her relief, he snatched the terrifying choice back out of her hands.

He opened his eyes and rasped, 'Do it. Hurry.'

His painfully-uttered words catapulted her into action. In less than two minutes, she had inserted a needle into his vein and started antivenom dripping through the tube. Another check of his vitals showed that his pulse rate was slowing and his breathing was becoming strident and shallow. Each tiny inward and outward move-ment of his chest appeared painful.

'Hold on, please, Alex, hold on. I have to get you into the ambulance.'

His deathly pallor and the clench of muscles across his face proved that he hung on by a mere thread. It took a Herculean effort and a terrifying amount of time to tug him onto a blanket, but if he passed out completely she'd have no chance of shifting him. So she talked, nagged, and forced him to stay alert. More importantly, to stay alive.

'Stay with me, Alex, please. I can't do this without you. I need your help. I need you alive.'

He helped her as much as he could and gave praise in a low monotone. 'Doing great. Panic... uses energy. Calm.'

She checked the color on his fingertips, made sure the anti-venom flowed in a slow steady drip, and reassured him. 'I'm going to get you there. You're going to be fine because I won't let you die. I swear it!'

By using the heavy-duty blanket, she dragged and maneuvered his large body, plus his IV tubing and bag, onto the floor of the ambulance. Alex used his legs a ton of willpower, and sheer brute strength to help her tumble him in a clumsy heap onto the stretcher.

'Strap me.'

She nodded and did as he ordered. Three firm belts, lashed at intervals across his shivering body, secured him to the stretcher. On the trip back to town, the ambulance's bumps and sways would be agonizing and cause him incredible pain. The strapping, and his elevated limb, prevented large volumes of blood from pumping through the infected area and carrying it to the rest of his body because once venom reached his vital organs, his chances would diminish rapidly. If she prevented the poison reaching his heart, Alex might have a chance, a slim one but at least a chance.

'Tape the IV,' he muttered.

She nodded again before strapping the bag to the pole and to the sides supports wherever she could so the anti-venom dripped with a measured consistency. Or at least as steadily as could be managed in the back of a swaying vehicle. The charge of adrenaline, plus the nervous energy she'd used, had exhausted her and she slumped to her knees beside his stretcher.

His eyes stayed shut but he turned his head a fraction nearer her ear. She leaned closer to catch his whispered words. 'Drive. Carefully.'

Clinging to the comforting idea he remained coherent enough to issue orders, she leant forward to press a light kiss onto his clammy forehead.

'I will, sweetheart. Stay still. And, please, please, don't die.'

A horrible moment of silence followed during which she truly believed she'd lost him, but he dragged his eyes open. He stared, eyes full of regrets and farewell before they sagged shut, and his words hissed out. 'I'm sorry.'

'No, no, no. Don't you dare say that. I won't let you. Not now. I need you, Alex. Stay alive for me. Promise!'

She gripped his fingers and willed him to listen. His eyes flickered open and he blinked acknowledgement. Her sob of relief echoed over-loudly in the cramped space, but she managed to swallow down the real cries threatening to rise and escape. Bending over his chest, she murmured the same words she'd repeated a thousand times in her lonely bed, too low for him to hear, though voicing her feelings comforted her.

'And I promise to get you there safely, because I love you.'

9

The drive back into the township was the most harrowing hour of Kristie's life. Her neck ached from swiveling between the road and the mirror and she nearly cried with relief when she finally drove into the hospital grounds. She'd radioed ahead so the instant the ambulance pulled to a halt the staff swung into action. Within a short time, Alex was admitted to a high care bed where the relief doctor, Luke, resplinted his arm and supported it in a sling strung high above his bed. His vital statistics were unstable, which worried all the staff but made Kristie frantic.

To lose Alex would be like cutting out her heart.

Maxine, the registered nurse on duty and one of Alex's best friends, worked beside his bed and made him comfortable. Although Kristie appreciated the extra attention Alex received from his old friends, she was acutely aware that the staff had no reason to think her entitled to the same privileges. By keeping their relationship a secret, she'd robbed herself of any legitimate reason to linger but, oh how she longed to. Damn it, she wanted to be in there with them, fussing and hovering. Instead, she stiffened her spine and walked away.

Work would keep her mind focused on the rest of the hospital and away from that particular room. She restocked the ambulance and ensured enough staff were flu-free to work for the next two shifts, but beyond routine jobs she could scarcely function. Until Alex's observations improved, she couldn't relax.

As she went past Luke at the door to Alex's room, she sketched a nod, but Luke stopped her with a hand on her arm. 'Kristie, are you okay? You should be in bed as well.'

'I'm fine, Luke. Only tired.'

'You did an incredible job out there. Grace and Jimmy are doing okay in the district hospital. Jimmy's heart attack was from a blocked artery so he'll be sent to the city for an operation. And Grace's ankle has been set.'

'Thank goodness.'

'You saved Alex's life. If you hadn't started the antivenom so quickly, his chances of surviving would have been very slim.'

Alex's voice, scratchy and unexpected, startled them. 'You mean ... I'm ... alive.'

Luke moved to Alex's bedside and leaned over and put his stethoscope to Alex's chest, listening to his breathing and his heart sounds. He stood back and grinned.

'Welcome back to the land of the living, mate.' He pointed to where she hovered near the door. 'You owe Kristie big-time for keeping your stubborn hide intact.'

Luke put his hand on the pulse point on Alex's inner wrist and looked up at the wall clock while he counted the beats, a blessing for Kristie because neither of the men could see her and notice her tears of relief.

'Right now your observations are stable,' Luke said, 'but we'll check every fifteen minutes. Brown snakes inject much more poison than others. You'll need more doses of antivenom.'

'Luke,' Alex rasped, grabbing his friend's arm. 'Big... problem.' He stopped to suck in a deep breath. 'Had snake bite. Before.'

'I know. Luckily Maxine remembered. I tried to check your chart, but it seems to have vanished. Lost in the files somewhere.'

'Ring. Research. Centre.' Alex gasped, but then stopped again to rest. 'Second time bites.'

'I've already spoken to them. They've suggested you may need the full four vials of CSL Brown Snake Anti-venom intravenously. That should reverse any chance of developing severe coagulopathy. If you're working out in the paddocks, the last thing you want is a bleeding disorder. Every time you get a scratch, or cut yourself, you'd be back in here. Problem is, while we're pumping it into your system, there's a high risk you'll go into anaphylactic shock. Anti-venom overload. So, my friend, looks like you'll be spending more time in a hospital bed.'

'Damn. Thought I'd finished being a patient.' After a brief pause to catch his breath, Alex said, 'But you're right. Bloody disaster to have a bleeding problem. Especially if I'm working cattle. Or a two-hour horse ride from home. How much time?'

'Strict bed rest for forty-eight hours. Probably a week in hospital. We'll do daily checks on your blood levels. Then a few more days hanging around town.'

Kristie had slumped into the chair by the door when Alex had first roused and could now see his horrified expression. She stiffened, ready for the argument he was certain to present to Luke, but to her surprise, he glanced towards her before nodding agreement.

'And, Kristie,' Luke said, before he walked out of the room, 'you're exhausted. I'm ordering you straight to bed.'

She hauled herself upright, accepting the truth behind Luke's diagnosis when every muscle in her body screamed exhaustion, but before she could will her legs to drag her towards bed, Alex stopped her.

'How... do you... feel?'

She gave a short laugh and swiped at her eyes with the back of her hand. 'Shouldn't I be asking you that?'

'We need to talk about–'

'Alex!' The high-pitched squeal from the doorway startled them. 'Thank goodness you're alive. I was out of mind with worry the entire drive in here.'

A beautiful blond in her early forties rushed into the room on a cloud of expensive perfume. Her designer jeans clung like a second skin and a fire-engine red silk shirt, knotted at her waist and with a slashed cleavage, exposed a large expanse of tanned skin.

Kristie glanced at her own filthy clothes, shuddered, and scrubbed an ineffectual hand over the dust laden creases of her uniform. She reached up to smooth her hair but stopped with her hand midair. If she had a million years, she couldn't compete with the blond bombshell who ignored her to brush past her and drape herself over Alex's chest.

'Eliza,' Alex repeated several times in an attempt to interrupt the stream of non-stop female chatter.

Kristie slipped out of the room unnoticed and leaned against the corridor wall. She blocked her ears, already guessing the woman's identity and not wanting to listen to any more platitudes from the woman she thought of as Alex's wicked stepmother. Unfortunately, the bed allocated for critically ill patients was directly outside her office and in closest view of the nursing staff.

Ten minutes of listening to Eliza's over-anxious and endless monologue set Kristie's teeth on edge and a dull pain throbbed at the base of her head, like the persistent pack of a woodpecker into her skull. As soon as she rostered enough staff to record Alex's observations every fifteen minutes, she'd disappear. Her main goal was to grab some overdue sleep. Not to run away, but to maintain a professional distance between she and Alex.

If only she could convince herself her disappearing act had nothing to do with the sharp sting of jealousy, she experienced each time Eliza called Alex 'darling' in her whining tone.

The next day, Alex stared at the ceiling above his bed. He was worried, very worried, but not about his own medical problems. From his central position in the ward, he could track the activities of all the nursing staff, especially Kristie's. Her afternoon nap yesterday had lasted for four hours, after which she'd eaten a meagre snack at her desk and then worked an evening shift. Now, at ten o'clock in the morning, she hadn't appeared. The staff's heavy workload wasn't what worried him, as Maxine covered his room and four other patients while Lee, the other registered nurse, efficiently managed the others.

'Maxine, don't you think someone should check on Kristie?'

'Alex, that's the fourth time You've asked in an hour. Lee checked her room and she was sleeping like a log.' She eyed him with suspicion. 'What is it with you two, anyway? I know you met in Brisbane. Is there something you're not telling me?'

Maxine had attended school with him and they'd travelled together to boarding school on the train each year, so she felt free to pry into his business as only an old time friend would. However, until Kristie took a pregnancy test and was ready to make her own announcements, he wouldn't discuss their relationship.

'We spent a long night at the plane. Then she dealt with my snake bite. She looked exhausted. Has she eaten anything this morning?'

Maxine grinned. 'Just how close did you two get in Brisbane?'

Long experience told him Maxine wouldn't stop until she unearthed the truth.

'After you check on Kristie–'

'I'm here now, Maxine.' Kristie's voice from the door startled them both. 'Just checking you're okay.'

His shoulders sagged in relief. 'Are you okay? You need something substantial to eat. And plenty of fluids.'

Two pairs of female eyes swiveled towards him and two faces held identical looks of utter disbelief. Maxine appeared goggle-eyed at the possibility of gathering juicy gossip. Kristie's expression said she either wanted the ground to open up and swallow her whole, or she wanted to put her hands around his neck and squeeze.

Better to avoid looking at her and speak to Maxine. 'What? Can't a hospital doctor inquire about a staff member's health?'

Maxine's grin widened until it threatened to split her face in two. 'This is too delicious for words. I think our hard-nosed Doctor Ryan is smitten.'

Kristie, head down, muttered something about food and scuttled from the room. He glared at Maxine. 'You embarrassed her.'

'Me? You did that all by yourself.' She glanced at the door through which Kristie had disappeared as if the devil chased her. 'But a word of warning. She's really nice and from the little she's said, she's had a hard life. We wouldn't want to see her hurt.'

'What makes you think I'm going to hurt her?'

'I saw the way you looked at her. Like you wanted to swallow her in one big gulp.'

'Your imagination is running away with you, as usual.'

'When you first brought Monica home, you looked at her the same way. Look how badly that ended.'

'It's different with Kristie.'

'Come on, Alex. I know you too well. You've already slept with her, haven't you?

'I'm not–' No point denying anything as Max could read him far too well.

'If I've noticed something going on between you two, so will other people. Like the not-so-delightful Eliza.'

Max loathed Eliza and her hold over the Ryan family and expressed her opinion. Loudly and often. She joked she'd never become romantically involved with Alex because the thought of having Eliza as a stepmother made her shudder.

'Did Eliza say something yesterday?'

'I wasn't on duty, but Lee overheard Eliza talking to Kristie.'

Maxine slipped into the chair beside his bed and leaned closer. She may be a gossip, but they'd shared a close bond since discovering as children they both suffered the consequences of living with a domineering single parent father.

'Eliza made a beeline for Kristie after she left you. You must have said something to alert her another prospective bride loomed on the horizon. She's never wasted any time when she wants to frighten away your girlfriends.'

He gave a dry laugh. 'She's never frightened you. But then, you were always too stubborn to be my girlfriend.'

'Too choosy.' She flashed him a saucy grin. 'My being friends with you was enough to give Eliza palpitations because my father's property isn't big enough to make me suitable as a Ryan. Still, your dear stepmother loves to cause problems between us, and she did her best to get rid of Monica.'

'Eliza made a point of telling me how much she admired Monica.'

'Hah! To your face. Behind your back she told the whole town Monica wouldn't last a month on Undulla. And she made a big deal out of telling Monica how hard life was so far away from civilization. Believe me, Eliza is one of the reasons Monica dumped you.'

He frowned, although in truth the idea had been niggling at the back of his mind for some time. Max's character judgments were astute and he only regretted not trusting her instinctive dislike of Monica. If he'd believed Max's assessment, he'd never have gone so far as becoming engaged to Monica. Never have let his feelings become so involved and therefore the disappointment so much harder to swallow.

'How do you know all this and I don't?'

She rolled her eyes. 'Well, duh! Men can't see beyond a woman's pretty face and big boobs. Women know these things.'

'And you know Eliza said something to Kristie?'

'I know if Eliza discovers your interest in Kristie, she'll do whatever she can to dispose of her. Railroad her out of town. And she's very cozy with some of the older hospital board members.'

After Maxine left, he returned to his contemplation of the ceiling. He'd suspected Eliza played on Monica's increasing fear of living full-time in the outback, but then their engagement had shattered and Eliza's involvement became a moot point. But if she interfered between he and Kristie, she'd soon learn he wasn't about to be manipulated.

She'd become over-confident with her tactics of shaming him into handing over the property to her son would work and he'd allowed her to think there was a chance of that happening, but only because it was too soon to force Ben to stand up to his own mother. He'd let those decisions slide until Ben finished at university and could decide for himself where his interests lay without Eliza dictating her own needs and wants.

His father's main interest in him had been as an heir to take over Undulla and carry on the Ryan tradition and he wasn't naive enough to believe Eliza's interest was anything more than ensuring her expensive lifestyle continued. Monica had viewed him as a well-heeled rung on the social climbing ladder in the city, never as a country doctor. Though he mightn't be able to accept everything Kristie believed as true, he did know that what they'd shared in Brisbane had been real and she hadn't been ruled by who, or what, he was but in him as a man. Her truly wanting him had felt good, very good.

For the next seven days, Alex fell into a pattern of resting and testing while Luke insisted he remain in bed and under strict observation. Two minor episodes of adverse drug reaction after his second antivenom infusion had sent the staff into a minor panic and, after that, Luke's instructions were for even stricter bed rest and frequent monitoring. Knowing nurses considered doctors to be the worst patients, he tried to comply and show an upbeat attitude, despite the inactivity making him want to scream with frustration. Although, he did reconcile himself to Luke's restrictions for one reason. Being confined to bed gave him plenty of time to watch Kristie work.

During the day she ignored him, tackling administrative jobs and helping with patient care. Two old men, both in their eighties and permanent residents of the hospital, adopted her as their personal darling and frequently, Bert or Ernie, as they were nicknamed, would summons her as she bustled past. No matter how busy, she always spared them a moment or two of her time. When staff was short and the ward busy, she became his nurse, so teasing her, when she maintained a professional distance, became the only bright spot in his long day.

'Nurse Donaldson,' he called for the fourth time in an hour. Nobody used formal titles in a ten-bed bush hospital, so this had become their private game.

'Yes, Doctor Ryan.' Her emphasis on his title in return amused him, her attempt at keeping him at arm's length. 'Is there something I can do to make you more comfortable?'

He snorted. 'I can think of a lot of things. None suitable for a hospital ward.'

By her sharp intake of breath and her quick glance towards the doorway, she grasped his meaning. Her tongue flicked out to moisten her dry lips and his body reacted, tightened, readied.

He shook his head. Amazing, yet reassuring to know a week of drugs hadn't diminished his instant sexual reaction. He resigned himself to another night of lustful thoughts which left him tossing and turning until Luke threatened to prescribe a sleeping pill, although a pill wasn't going to fix this particular problem. Only having a certain warm nurse wrapped around him would ease this sort of pain.

Instead, he envisioned swimming in a freezing water hole or trekking up Mt Everest, anything to regain control of his treacherous body. If Kristie noticed his muscles hardening and his breath coming faster every time she leaned over him, she didn't comment. Yet she couldn't be so oblivious that she didn't notice him suck in a lungful of her scent each time she stretched up to the pole where his IV bag hung.

He breathed in her scent as a released prisoner breathes in fresh free air. 'Roses,' he muttered.

'What?'

'Today you smell like roses. Yesterday it was vanilla.'

'Do you have nothing better to do than smell me, Doctor Ryan?'

As she worked around him taking his blood pressure and temperature, he smiled. 'As a matter of fact, Nurse Donaldson, smelling you is the highlight of my entire day. I spend the night trying to guess which fragrance you'll wear the next morning. Traditional roses or an exotic musk.'

She rolled her eyes. 'Please, Doctor Ryan. Go back to reading your medical journals. Far more interesting than a guessing game on my perfume.'

As she turned and walked to the door, he couldn't resist a final prod. 'Far more interesting studying anatomy in person than in a journal, Nurse Donaldson.'

Her loud gasp was music to his ears, although mentioning her anatomy only heightened his frustration at spending another day in this bed with only imagination and dreams for company. Each evening, when her official hours were over, Kristie sat at his bedside and talked, relieving his frustration with confinement. Any mention of what lay between them, or her possible condition, was banned.

Kristie made it clear she wouldn't discuss any of that here, at his bedside, in a public hospital, and because he was so pathetically grateful to have her company, he abided by her rules, for now. Their conversation consisted mainly of hospital problems which he could discuss from a medical point of view and as a hospital administrator. Her voice soothed his restlessness, in contrast to the irritation he felt each afternoon when he endured Eliza's smothering visits.

Dawn to dusk working hours allowed him to escape from her complaints and clinging attitude, only having to appear for a brief time over a polite dinner. After his accident six month earlier and his father's passing, she'd taken over more of the day to day decision-making around the homestead, but there was no way he would allow her the final say on their thousands of acres of cattle grazing land.

Yet, he was still being coerced into managing Undulla when all he really wanted was to practice medicine again.

10

B y the fifth morning of his confinement to bed, Alex was going stark raving mad from the forced inactivity. Erratic blood levels meant Luke refused to release him from this suffocating prison. No, that wasn't fair. Every decision Luke made had been the correct one. If the shoe was on the other foot, he'd take no chances with an unstable snake bite patient either.

'Alex, you're like a caged lion.' Luke checked his observation chart and frowned.

'No bloody wonder.'

'And you're as cranky as one too. I ordered bed rest for good reason.'

'Small children get cranky. I'm a frustrated doctor.'

Luke rolled his eyes. 'Maybe if you're extra nice to Kristie, she'll agree to sit with you more today. It seems to be the only time you're calm.'

'I've been calm for five damn days. I'm dying of boredom.'

'The more agitated you become, the more your blood pressure rises. More chance of adverse reaction to the anti-venom. One more episode like yesterday's, when your blood pressure skyrocketed, and

I'll send you off to the city. You'll be strapped to a bed for another two weeks.'

Alex grunted. He'd already wasted far too much of this year as a patient. He looked at Kristie. 'If I improve my temperament, will you stay and talk to me? Stop me climbing the walls.'

Luke nodded. 'Bore him to tears with hospital budgets until he settles down.' He tapped his pen on the chart. 'I really don't like this. His observations are all over the place.'

'Fine. I'll stay until Maxine finishes morning treatments. Then she can endure his royal grumpiness.'

'First, his royal grumpiness is in the room. Second, I don't want Maxine.' He pointed at Kristie. 'I want you.'

Kristie, hand on her hips, echoed his belligerent tone. 'Well, I don't want you because you're far too difficult. You should know better than to cause trouble for the staff.'

Luke threw up his hands and shook his head. 'I'm leaving. You two can fight it out.'

Alex sighed. 'Luke, Kristie, I'm sorry. The damn medication is making me irritable.'

'I know.' Luke said. 'But you either rest or I order extra sedatives.'

Luke left and Kristie looked at him, brow raised. 'What's it to be? Calm down, or take a pill?'

He lay back and slowed his breathing, relaxed his muscles. 'I'm calm, placid, resting like a well fed baby.'

Kristie pulled a chair up to the bed and began to talk in a low monotonous tone. 'I'm working on staff budgets for the next twelve months. But I need to cut five thousand off the wages bill somewhere to make it balance.'

He threw his arm over his eyes and moaned. 'Luke was only kidding when he said to bore me to death with budgets. Can't you talk about something more interesting.'

From under his arm, he watched Kristie's bowed head and shoulders shake. The witch was laughing at him. 'It's either budgets or watching me knit.'

He lifted his arm and peered at her. 'Knit?'

'I knit to relax. You should try it.'

'For relaxation, I perform ten hour surgeries. '

'Not lately, you don't.'

He flinched. 'Thanks for reminding me.'

She took his hand, pressed his fingers. 'I'm sorry. I know you miss surgery. Medicine. All of it.'

He pulled his fingers from her grip and turned his gaze to the wall, away from her pity.

'I do miss it. Since my father's death, I've been needed at Undulla. But out there at the plane, we were doing what's really important. Saving lives.'

'Time you went back to work then. Full time. '

Her words, straight to the jugular as always, jolted him. He turned to stare at her. 'Why do you say that?'

'Because you're a doctor. You need to work to feel whole. I saw how good you were at the plane crash.'

'No more than you. You're a very capable nurse.'

She smiled, the first genuine smile of happiness she'd given him. He'd missed it, missed her joy for living. When she smiled, everyone around her felt better.

'I'd better go and get my knitting. These sort of serious conversations will make you more restless. Besides, you'll have time to make those decisions after you go home. After you talk to Ben again.'

When she left to fetch her knitting, he followed her orders and relaxed his body but allowed his thoughts to race. She'd nailed his problem; the real reason bed rest drove him crazy. Not because he missed ruling thousands of acres of property, despite how much he loved the freedom of riding across his cattle station. No, his fingers itched to pick up a scalpel. His hands needed to operate again. Dipping his toes back into medicine this week stirred a deeper yearning.

To do that, he'd have to hire a station manager who'd have to be strong enough to resist his stepmother's interference. Even though his father had been dead for several months, he could imagine the sting of his father's wrath. His father refused to admit being a doctor was as worthwhile as building a pastoral empire. Saving other people was lower on his importance scale than enriching the Ryan family.

Kristie returned with her knitting but he closed his eyes and pretended to be asleep. She was too astute by far. The last months had drained him. Straight after seeing his mate lying beside him on the road and being too injured himself to save him, all he'd wanted was to crawl into a hole and lick his wounds. She'd poked and prodded and not let him retreat into his shell then, and it seemed she wasn't about to now. Plus, his priorities had shifted. Any previous ambitions mellowed. If he returned to a large city hospital, he'd decided to specialize in trauma surgery, not the more glamorous and name-building surgeries driving him before.

Problem was, he hadn't resolved everything. Not made the hardest choices. He heard Kristie turn away from his bed and walk back to the door and breathed a sigh of relief. Enough soul-searching for today, openly at least. Yet, as soon as she left the room felt empty, deflated, and lonely.

From his position next to the nurse manager's office, he had a bird's eye view of all the action so he noticed every time Kristie rushed to the bathroom each morning. Then, like an overanxious obstetrician or an obsessed fool, he counted off the minutes until she re-emerged. This time, when she tried to hurry past his room, he called her over and unable to ignore a patient, she obeyed his summons. Her face was whiter than the sheet he lay on and when he reached for her wrist to take her pulse, she slapped at his hand with shaking fingers.

'Don't touch me,' she whispered, head swiveling from side to side to see if anyone else was around. 'People will notice.'

He took her hand again and slid his fingers over the pulse in her wrist. Her washed-out pallor and the sight tremble of her arm he felt made her appear vulnerable, fragile, and raised his protective instincts.

'Nurses are observant. Don't you think they'll already have put two and two together?'

'Nobody has mentioned anything.'

'You've thrown up every morning regular as clockwork.'

'Are you timing me?'

'Have you done a pregnancy test?'

'No!' She wrenched her hand back.

'Although, from the amount of time you spend in the bathroom, it's certain to be positive.'

'Stop harassing me.'

'I'm worried for you. About you.'

'Fine. I'll do a test. If it's positive, you'll be the first to know.'

When she hurried away, head down and shoulders slumped, guilt drilled a hole in his gut. All hell was about to break loose and he'd instigated it. Kristie's single mother status was certain to embarrass the more straight-laced board members and they'd either push for her resignation, or expect her to make arrangements to appear more respectable. Perhaps even suggesting a reunion with the father to satisfy the conservative element of the town.

If he was smart, he'd avoid stirring that particular hornet's nest or he'd wipe any chance of her sitting with him and stopping him going stir crazy. He laughed at the irony. Despite his constantly harassing Luke about being discharged, he wanted to stay in hospital. How crazy was that?

Kristie perched on the rim of the bath and stared at the test stick in her hand. Watched it change color. Positive. She didn't know whether to laugh or cry. In some ways, pregnancy was a dream come true. Yet in others, a disaster. Alex was about to become a father, whether he accepted the possibility or not. She'd transferred to the outback at her brother's urging, hoping two rational adults could have a face to face discussion about their relationship. Hoping for a new future.

She'd already fallen in love with the town and, with or without Alex's presence in her life, had decided she'd love to make the valley her home, though she predicted the troublesome hospital board would be outraged when their new Director of Nursing applied for maternity leave. They'd be forced to allow her to stay until a replacement could be found, but then what?

Unless Alex opened his mind to the possibility of their baby, her plans for the future needed revising. She pressed a hand to her still flat stomach and pictured her growing baby, imagined a family of her own. Caring for her mother and supervising her brother had consumed every spare moment and drained every ounce of energy, forcing her to forfeit her fiancée and the dream of children that went with him.

Their father deserted she and Steven when they were small children, so after her mother died she'd goaded her only living relative into hanging onto life, not being able to bear the thought of losing him as well. She'd pushed him to stand strong, to fight his life-threatening addiction, and when he'd regained enough of his old happier personality to attempt living a normal life again, she'd been ecstatic. Every day, she prayed his girlfriend's influence would keep him drug free.

Although she was never naïve enough to believe Steven cured, understanding only too well the chances of him relapsing. Plus, he required life-time supervision of his medication and his mental state as she'd witnessed firsthand many other residents in his drug rehab house regress, either from bouts of depression from withdrawal or being unable to cope with real life. Thankfully, Steven called her relocation a journey of exploration for both of them, while he tested his new-found independence without the crutch of the rehab house. And without her daily visits.

Her darling brother had promised if her appointment became permanent, he and Gina would also relocate to the valley. The three of them could start a new life away from Steven's city drug sources and shake off the stigma of addict preventing him from getting honest employment. And there would have been the extra bonus of a baby, a niece or nephew for Steven to concentrate on. Even while the color on her pregnancy stick grew brighter, all thoughts of them realizing their collective dream in this wonderful town grew dimmer. Every time she took a step forward, towards what she wanted most, a giant hand reached out an shoved her backwards. And right now, the thing she'd wanted most lay close by, so close she could almost touch him, awaiting news of a child he believed belonged to some other man.

Dropping her head in her hands, she took a few moments to wallow in self-pity and allowed her tears of regret to fall before she accepted the idea of a lifetime alone. Though she wouldn't be alone, she'd have a new person to care for and to love.

She scrubbed her face, stiffened her spine, and strode towards Alex's room.

11

A lex watched Kristie as she approached his bed. 'It's positive, isn't it?'

A frown creased her forehead and her eyes were unfocused. 'Yes. I'm pregnant.'

Neither of them spoke while she stared off into the distance, emotions chasing each other across her face. She tilted her head to the side as she did when thinking over a problem, but then her mouth turned up at the corners and a smile grew across her face until her face lit up with blossoming joy.

'I'm pregnant. And I'm happy about it.' She rubbed tiny circles over her stomach and her eyes glazed with the universal other-worldly realization of impending motherhood. 'Very happy.'

He'd witnessed the same holding-their-breath awe on plenty of expectant mothers and fathers when they'd first learned their news. Their faces radiated anticipation, joy, and then acceptance. Wanting to at least bask in her glow, he reached for her hand.

'I'm glad, for your sake, if it's what you want.'

'I do. I want it so very much.'

He drew a deep breath, kept his grip on her fingers light. 'You can tell me now. Whose baby is it?'

Snatching her hand away, she stepped back and glared, as if he'd taken a knife to her body and not merely been cruel enough to deflate her euphoria like yesterday's party balloon. Her shoulders sagged as her breath whooshed out on a long sigh. All her previous animation evaporated.

'It's mine.' Her eyes met his, her gaze fierce, yet her voice quavered.

He mentally kicked himself. A decent man wouldn't spoil her moment of elation.

'It could have been your baby, too.' She spoke towards her stomach as her hand gently circled there again. 'But, my beautiful baby, you and I are going to be a family.' She shot him another look, disappointed, angry, and determined. 'We don't need anyone else.'

He flinched, her words hitting like a fist to his gut, and turned away from the accusation in her eyes. Everything he'd said had been raw, painful, truths. The chances of him creating Kristie's baby were a million to one. So why, when she absolved him from any involvement, did he yearn for it?

He swallowed past the lump wedged in his throat. 'I do care about you, Kristie. I'll help you do whatever you think best.'

'I have to think about the future.' She touched her fingers to her stomach, as if unable to believe a small being already grew there. 'Our future.'

'Your plans will need to include the baby's father.' As he slumped back on his pillows, he expected her to renew her denial of being involved with another man.

Instead, her eyes filled with tears and she visibly drooped. 'No.' Her voice was a whisper. 'Not if the father isn't interested.'

She spun around and blundered to the door, almost hitting the post in her rush. Without thinking, he threw his legs over the side of the bed and came to his feet but the intravenous tube, attached to a steel pole, jerked him to an abrupt halt.

'Dammit, Kristie. Come back.' He kicked the four-pronged base of his drip pole and rattled the connections and tubing, hoping the noise might bring her back.

His temper nose-dived further when Eliza stepped into his room, having pressed back against the door jamb when Kristie pushed past her in the doorway. Typically, his delightful step-mother wasted no time twisting the knife in his already bleeding chest.

'Well, well. How entertaining. And how nauseating. So, your pathetic little nurse is really pregnant.'

'You listened?'

She gave her cat who'd swallowed the cream smile. 'Of course. Your engagement to Monica proved you're a typical male. Incapable of deciphering good from bad when it comes to scheming women.'

'Kristie,' he said through clenched teeth, 'is not scheming.'

She patted his hand, over where he'd clenched it in the sheet. 'On the contrary. I've good reason to believe she applied for this job for the sole purpose of stalking you.'

Instead of worrying him, her news comforted him. He'd allowed some of Eliza's earlier poisonous gossip and insinuations to worm into his mind and fester because Kristie had refused to tell him her true motives for turning up in his hometown. Deep down though, he'd never believed she'd come because of Mike. After all, she'd worked her first weeks in the director's position when Mike was away on his honeymoon.

He glanced at Eliza, studied her smug expression. 'Why do you think she's stalking me?'

'I have my sources.'

He snorted. 'You mean Rob Mason, your faithful errand boy. Did you have to sleep with him before he'd show you the minutes from the last board meeting? The one where Kristie's application was discussed.'

Eliza studied her red-painted nails and shrugged. 'Does it matter?'

'Yes, it matters. It's unethical, and illegal.'

She looked at him with eyes wide, fierce, and perhaps a little crazy. 'I do whatever is necessary to protect my family. The same way I've always done.'

'You mean you interfere in people's lives to protect Ben's inheritance?'

'I'm a mother. I don't have to explain myself, or my methods.'

'Did you use those same methods to convince Monica she'd kill her career if she lived out here?'

She shrugged again, the deep slash of her silky singlet slipping to reveal the top of perfectly formed breasts. He closed his eyes, trying to forget the outlandish amount of money his father had paid for her enhancement, and knowing every move she made was contrived to display them at best advantage. More and more over the last few weeks she'd been displaying them for his benefit. Surely, she couldn't truly imagine there could be anything between them?

The thought of intimacy with his cold stepmother made him shudder and for that reason he'd dismissed her little tricks as her normal unconscious flirtatious mannerisms. Not a deliberate attempt to entice her stepson into her bed. It wasn't their age difference horrifying him as Eliza was closer to his age than his fathers. Her ruthless ambition concerning her two children was Eliza's only softer feature. Otherwise, he likened bedding her to spending a night in a snake's cage.

'I may have exaggerated a little when I told Monica how tiresome it is living so far from civilization.'

'Oh, come on. From the day you married my father, You've had a plane at your disposal to visit the city or to holiday at the beach.'

'I still did you an enormous favor getting rid of Monica. She was nothing but a social climbing little upstart. Certainly not good enough to be a Ryan. You should thank me.'

Her unapologetic gall left him speechless. She'd always been manipulative but recently her obsessions had turned her into an evil witch. Kristie and Maxine had both recognized the large heaping of guilt Eliza had piled on him for her own selfish ends. He'd allowed her free rein for far too long.

'But there is one good thing about this.' Her self-satisfied smirk made his stomach churn. 'that ill-bred girl cannot possibly claim you have fathered her baby.' She walked her perfectly manicured nails in little steps down his arm, raising goose flesh. 'Because we all know you're incapable of performing the deed, don't we, my darling?'

He stiffened. 'And you never miss an opportunity to remind me, and everybody else, I'm damaged. Half a man.'

'Nonsense. Our new arrangements suit me perfectly. Ben continues the Ryan heritage, steps into your father's shoes, and you assist him. Undulla will grow even larger. Ben will be wealthier than your father.'

'You're talking as if the accident affected my mind as well as my body. I've never said Ben will take control. I'm still considering all the options.'

Her fingers, where they rested on his sheet, shook a little. He heard the catch in her breathing. But she trilled a small laugh. 'For a tiny second, I thought you were serious.'

'I am serious. Ben isn't ready and despite your efforts to unsettle me, I'm still in control. If you value your little luxuries and expect them to continue, you'd do well to remember that.'

Her eyes widened. Damn. It shocked him to realize how much he'd let things slide with her, how long he'd avoided confronting her. How much she'd assumed.

'And I may still marry someday.'

'No. Who would want you?'

'Is it so hard to imagine someone marrying me for something other than children? What about love?'

She narrowed her gaze. 'Don't be ridiculous. People of our station marry to join properties together. We marry for wealth and then hope love happens later.'

'I've got money and property. Now there's a chance I could have love, and a child.'

'Don't you dare even consider marrying that nurse to acquire her child. A child that's not even a Ryan. I forbid it.'

He sucked in a breath, held it, fought for control. 'Although I appreciate the many decisions you made for Undulla after my accident, you've no say in my personal life. I'll marry any time, or anyone, I want and you'll not interfere ever again. Do I make myself clear?'

Eliza refused to allow Alex's ridiculous ultimatum rattle her composure. Her plans for the future didn't include another woman living at Undulla House, unless it was one she handpicked to become Ben's wife. She'd rid the valley of the first prospective Mrs. Alex Ryan and the second would be dealt with this very day.

After explaining to Alex, she had business to attend to in town before she drove home, she forced herself to act out her exit scene in an unhurried fashion. He'd never guess from her outward performance of calm acceptance that inwardly she seethed over his arrogant treatment of her. She'd tasted real power when she'd controlled their estates by herself for those weeks and she'd not share that feeling with anyone but her son. Alex's role must remain as a valued family member, not the passer of the heritage Ben would become.

She drove directly from the hospital to the bank and invited her friend, Bob Mason, to lunch. Bob could coerce the board into rescinding the position of that interfering nonentity Kristie Donaldson and send her back to the city with her tail between her legs. Revealing cleavage, tight jeans, and a hand under their lunch table caressing his thigh would render Rob putty in her hand. Men were so incredibly easy to stage manage.

'Bob,' she purred, 'I am certainly not a prude. However, I was shocked to learn that the nurse caring for my darling step-son, while he is in such a vulnerable state, is a man-hunting wanton. She came here to chase not just one, but two doctors.' She pressed closer so Bob enjoyed the full thrust of her firm breasts against his arm. 'And she is soon to be a single mother.'

Bob gave a start of surprise. 'She hasn't mentioned any of this to the board.'

'The only thing to do is to lapse her contract before it becomes common knowledge that the board made a terrible error of judgment.'

'Work laws won't let us terminate her contract because of a pregnancy, Eliza.'

Irritated that Bob wasn't falling over himself to please her, she pushed her case. She slid her fingers in an arousing fashion up and down his thigh. 'But you must make it clear, darling, that our hospital has standards to uphold. I know it is considered last century morals, but the older generation of our town is conservative to a fault.'

Bob's hand covered Eliza's in encouragement as it stroked higher on his thigh. 'I'll take care of it immediately.'

'Thank you, Bob.' She squeezed just inches below his groin. 'You're a true friend to me.'

'You know that I want to be a lot more than just a friend, Eliza.'

Eliza, while happy to flaunt her femininity to get what she wanted, had no intention of narrowing her life to the world of a small town banker like Bob Mason. However, she smiled with false sincerity.

'Until you dispose of this threat to my family's safety, Bob, I shall be unable to rest. After our town is free of that grasping nurse, I'll gladly demonstrate my gratitude.'

12

Kristie did her best to avoid Alex for the next two days as she buzzed around the hospital. She solved problems, organized admissions and attended outpatient clinics with two visiting doctors. Becoming involved with many of the families in town delighted her, as she loved people, loved helping them. But at the back of her mind, her problems lingered. Alex's presence distracted her.

The town's populace valued their bush hospital and used every opportunity to give something back to the community. Today was blood donor day and forty people were on the list to donate in their once a month collection, the blood being sent for processing to the city. However, they were short one nurse, or doctor. As she walked to Alex's room to check his blood pressure, she caught the sound of arguing.

'Luke, I'm quite capable of inserting a few needles and collecting blood without overtaxing myself,' Alex said. 'If it will make you happier, I'll even stay seated while I do it.'

'Okay, but just remember that I'm only letting you do this under sufferance,' Luke reminded him. 'And only because we're so short staffed. You're not to do anything strenuous.'

From the door, Kristie watched Alex sketch a mock salute to his mate and grin. 'Gotcha, boss.'

Luke walked past her shaking his head. 'Hard- headed doctors will be the death of me.'

'I heard that,' Alex called from his bed. 'And don't forget, Luke, you're one of those hard-headed doctors.

Luke looked at Kristie and said, 'I'm going to get started. You can bring him down to the donor room as soon as he's had his observations checked. I'm not taking any risks until his blood tests are back to normal.'

For the next three hours, doctors and nurses worked in harmony until they heaved a collective sigh of relief when the last donor left the clinic. Whenever she wasn't required in the wards, Kristie dropped in to lend a hand. It was a blessing the afternoon was busy, as it left her no time to brood on her problems. So, when Luke called his question across the room, she froze, caught off guard and plunged into a moment of shock.

'Kristie and Maxine, you're off duty now so do you both want to donate blood?'

Before either of the women could reply, Alex answered. 'Not Kristie. She can't donate.'

Every eye spun to her as Luke asked, 'Why not?'

Kristie realized the moment of truth had arrived. Drawing a deep, steadying breath, she answered, 'Because I'm pregnant.' In the ensuing silence, Kristie glanced from one to the other, assimilating their guilty looks. 'You guys all knew, didn't you?'

The tension in the room dissipated as everyone spoke at once.

'Congratulations,' Maxine squealed.

'I knew it,' Mary added smugly. 'After four pregnancies, I can recognize morning sickness.'

Maxine grinned. 'We guessed by the number of mornings you ran to the bathroom, but we were waiting for you to tell us.'

Lee couldn't contain her excitement as she asked, 'When are you due?'

Kristie's mind reeled under the onslaught. She shook her head. 'I don't know,' she murmured, overwhelmed by all the attention.

Luke laid a comforting hand on her shoulder. 'We'd better do a scan, then. What do you say?'

She nodded, unable to speak. Tears threatened and she fought them back, not wanting to break down in front of them all.

Luckily, Luke took pity on her. 'Max, get yourself ready to have your blood drawn. And ladies, you have other patients waiting.' He shooed Lee and Mary away. 'Now Kristie, what about that scan?'

She opened her mouth but once again Alex answered for her. 'Good idea, Luke. Let's go.'

'Hey, excuse me.' She swung around to glare at Alex. 'I am in the room and I can make decisions for myself.' Turning her back to Alex, she spoke directly to Luke. 'I'll have a scan done in the morning, if that's okay, because now I'd like you to see Mrs. Williams. She's still in a lot of pain.'

Luke shrugged. 'Sure. I'll see her now and we'll do that scan after out-patients tomorrow.' He turned to Alex. 'Thanks for your help, mate. I owe you. Couldn't have drawn everyone's blood without you.' He nodded towards where Maxine was getting ready to give her own blood donation. 'Can you just finish up with Maxine?'

'No problem.'

Before Alex could say anything more, Kristie scuttled away to Mrs. Williams bedside. Anything to avoid Alex's lecture.

Alex watched her leave, knowing she was running away before he questioned her about her scan, her pregnancy, or her future. Maxine studied him in silence, unusual for her. He inserted the needle and connected the tubing, making sure the blood flowed well. The medical procedure taken care of, he leaned back and braced himself for Maxine's interrogation.

'Alex, you need to fix this.'

He gave a resigned sigh. 'I don't suppose it'll do any good to tell you that it isn't my problem to fix.'

'The fact remains that Kristie's pregnant, and someone is the father. I'm not asking if it's you. Only you and Kristie know that and until she wants to tell us more, we'll respect her privacy.'

'Good idea.'

'But a word of advice, Alex. That guy she nearly married hurt her when he left. When the going got tough with her family problems, he dumped her.'

'I didn't do that. I didn't dump Kristie over any family problems.'

'Don't forget, I was at Mike's wedding too. From the story I heard that morning, you didn't for one-minute blame Mike for kissing Kristie, but you blamed Kristie for kissing Mike. You turned your back on her and didn't even give her a chance to explain. Despite that, she still found the courage to come here, to try again. So now, if you care about her–'

'I do care. I care what happens to her, and her baby. But what am I supposed to do?'

'You need to show her that you have the courage to stick by her, no matter what.'

'I don't know if I can do that. Accept another man's baby, I mean. There are still too many unanswered questions between us.'

'Alex, you and I both know the chances of you having a baby of your own might be slim–'

'Less than slim, Max.'

'Okay, your sperm count was low after your accident, but I still think you should be retested. I told you that all along.'

'Why? So Eliza can ridicule me even more? Insinuate that I'm no longer a man? Tell the whole town. Again.'

Maxine's eyes clouded with tears of pity and he couldn't stand it. He placed his hand over hers. 'Sorry, Max. I didn't mean to take my frustration out on you. It wasn't fair. You're a good friend. But I've resigned myself to never having children.'

Maxine shook her head. 'No, you're just being bloody stubborn. You love kids and you'll be an amazing father.'

'You're forgetting that Kristie's baby already has a father. And it's not likely to be me.'

'Well, whoever it is, the father I mean, and I'm still not convinced it isn't you–'

'It's not!'

'Well, you're the one who's here, with her, near her. She came here to you, Alex. If you pass up this opportunity, a second chance to have a life with Kristie, you're a....a fool.'

He gave her a small smile. 'Just a fool? Is that the best you can do? You called me a lot worse than that when we were kids.'

She grinned. 'Okay, if you don't try again with Kristie, convince her to give you another chance, you're a damn stubborn, bull-headed idiot. Is that better?'

He had to laugh. 'Yeah, That's more like the best friend I know and love.'

Alex closed his eyes and bowed his head, waiting for the blood transfusion to finish. Maxine had always called a spade a spade, but was she right this time? Had he been stupid? Blinded by past hurts to the truth? For the last few weeks, he'd questioned his sanity enough times. For an intelligent man, he'd reacted with as much finesse as a rejected adolescent the day after the wedding. In his saner moments, he'd regretted his discourtesy to Kristie. She hadn't deserved that level of antagonism from him.

His over-the-top reaction had been a direct result of his still festering bitterness at being thrown over by a money hungry Monica. And if he was completely truthful, his rapidly increasing resentment that his stepmother felt entitled to regulate his life. Not to mention his initial apathy when he was grieving the death of his friend, which had left him wide open to Eliza's domination. He shook his head in disgust at himself. For the last six months, his emotions had been on a roller coaster ride of ups and downs and he had let things slide in his life, important things. Things that needed to be fixed.

Growing up on a vast cattle property, he'd never been afraid of hard work and in his climb to become one of the best surgeons in Australia, he'd never allowed minor hiccoughs to stop him. So even he was at a loss to comprehend why he'd recently evaded difficult decisions. But no more. Physically he was healed and mentally, he was prepared. Time to face down his demons. Time to start a new chapter in his life. And he knew now that without a strong woman sharing it with him, that new chapter would not be worth writing.

Maxine's blood donation was complete. He applied tape to her arm and they both stood, but he stopped her with a touch. 'max, thanks. Your diagnosis of my problem is spot on, as usual.'

She smiled, then stretched up to kiss his cheek. 'No problem. I've always loved interfering in your love life. Do you remember Maggie Tolster?'

'From the train? On the way home from boarding school?'

'Yeah. I knew you were working up the courage to kiss her, so I told her you had a severe strep throat. And if she caught it from you, she'd need injections of antibiotics every day for a week. And they'd hurt like hell.'

Once he recovered from his surprise, he threw back his head and laughed.

'No wonder she looked terrified whenever I came near her.'

'I did you a favor. She married Adam Jacobson for his family's name and prestige, then divorced him a year later and took all his money.'

'So, I owe you for that too.'

'Too?'

'Yeah, You've given me the nudge I needed, a none too gentle nudge mind you, to speak to Kristie about her future here. In the valley and at the hospital. If she wants to stay here and have the baby, I'll support her all the way.'

'Alex, speaking as a woman, I think she'll expect far more from you than a show of support at her workplace. She'll want you to stand strong bedside her when the town criticizes her for being an unwed mother.'

'Max, we may live in the bush, but we don't live in the dark ages. Single mothers are accepted everywhere.'

'We live in a small town. Small towns gossip. And gossip hurts. I just don't want to see Kristie hurt so badly that she flees town to escape the criticism. The staff here all like her. She's a great nurse. Knowledgeable and dedicated. We want to keep her here.'

'Keeping her here is not entirely up to me, Max. Others are involved. The hospital board for one. The baby's father for another.'

She patted his cheek where she had just kissed it. 'Do your best, Alex. Follow your heart. You always were the kindest person I know. Be kind to Kristie now. She needs you. The rest will sort itself out with time.'

'How did you get to be so wise?'

Maxine's eyes clouded over and her face contorted with pain. 'I've learned from experience.'

Alex considered what she'd said and remembered her own sad history. Maxine had returned to the bush after her husband and baby son were killed in a senseless accident with a drunk driver. 'Yeah, you have. You've had enough problems in your life. I can see why you sympathize with Kristie.'

He hugged Max and then let her go back to her nursing duties. With his mind in a whirl, he returned to his hospital room, for once glad of the peace he found there. Mulling over the afternoon's events, he finally reached a conclusion. Inactivity had never been part of his nature. If he wanted the future he had always dreamed of, with a family of his own, and being able to practice the medicine he loved, he needed to make better choices than he had recently. He needed to take action.

He reached for his buzzer and pressed, then lay back and waited. Just as he predicted, Kristie came running, as her office was closest to his bed and it was the first time, the only time, he'd called for help.

'What? What happened? Are you okay?'

She sounded out of breath and worried and he knew he should feel guilty for stressing a pregnant woman, but he didn't and he couldn't, not when he felt so pleased that she would still come running to assist him, despite how badly he'd treated her in the past.

He grinned. 'Have dinner with me?'

'What?' She looked confused. 'What did you say?'

'I asked you to have dinner with me, at the pub.'

She subsided into his bedside chair, hands clutched to her chest, and then he did feel guilty. 'You pressed your bell. I thought you'd had a relapse and all you wanted was to ask me to go to the pub with you? I thought it was an emergency.'

Despite her stunned disbelief, the smile refused to fade from his face as he gazed at her. 'It is an emergency. Luke's letting me out of here in the morning, provided I spend a couple of days in town, at the pub. So, I'll be alone, and bored, and I'll need someone to talk to.'

She shook her head. 'I can't believe you call that an emergency. You scared me half to death. I thought you were dying. Again.'

'I am dying. Dying of frustration and boredom. I need you to save me. You make me feel alive.' He was gratified to hear the small gasp of surprise she gave. 'Say yes, Kristie. It's just dinner. And we do need to talk.'

'Hah! The pub is the worst place to conduct a conversation, especially a private one. Everyone listens.' Her head dropped to her chest. She twisted her pen around and around in her hands. After a long silence, she raised her eyes to meet his. 'No, Alex, it's not a good idea. Word will have already spread that I'm pregnant. If you're seen out with me, people will assume things. Things you didn't want them to know about our relationship.'

'I don't care what they say. Let them talk.'

'Alex, a week ago you were horrified that the whole town already knew we'd met before in Brisbane. Nothing has changed, apart from the fact that I'm pregnant, and we both know how you feel about that.'

He laid his head back on the pillows and studied the ceiling. Kristie was correct. He'd made it clear that the baby she was carrying was the responsibility of its father, not him. 'I don't know how I feel.' He turned his head enough to meet her gaze. 'I only know that I miss talking to you, being with you. Can't we let that be enough, for now? Please?'

'And if people ask about the father of my baby, what do you want me to tell them?' she asked, tears collecting at the corners of her eyes.

He took a tissue and reached over to dab at her eyes. 'I'm sorry. I didn't mean to cause you more pain, I truly didn't . If people are crass enough to ask, tell them the truth.'

She shot to her feet, throwing her pen to the floor as she went. 'the truth! I tried to tell you the truth and you couldn't handle it, remember? You wouldn't believe me.'

'Damn it, Kristie, I'm trying here. But if I believe what you're telling me, if I let myself believe that there's the slightest possibility that your baby may be my baby, then someone has misled me. Or lied to me.'

'Lied? I don't understand.'

'About my tests from before.'

'And why is it harder to believe that may have happened than to trust what I'm saying to you?'

'Because there's only one person who could have done that. Luke was the doctor here when I was brought back to the valley after my accident. Luke, my friend, who has no reason to tell me something that isn't true.'

'Did you see the results yourself?'

He stared at her in disbelief. 'You can't be serious. Why would Luke lie to me?'

She made a distressed sound, halfway between a hiccough and a sob. 'I don't know.' She shook her head, making her hair fly around her face, the ends catching wetly in the tears that had started to fall in earnest. 'But please, Alex, if you still feel anything for me, for us and what we had, ask Luke. At least find out for sure. You owe me that much.'

He drew a deep breath and heaved it out on a sigh. 'Fine, you're right. I do owe you something. I know I reacted badly that day in Brisbane–'

Kristie gasped. 'Alex,' she murmured, her eyes filling with tears.

He slid his legs over the side of the bed and sat up, reaching for her hand. 'Kristie, I regret the way things turned out. I really do. I'd like to make a deal with you.'

'A deal,' she echoed with a puzzled frown, swiping a hand across her face and only managing to streak her face with more tears.

Instead of making her appear a disheveled mess as it would some women, her reddened face and puffy eyes only made her seem more vulnerable, more in need of his help. Hell, he would be a cruel man, totally vindictive, if he couldn't find a way to make a newly pregnant woman's life a little easier than this.

It was something he'd always done without thinking for his patients, especially the mothers of the children he operated on. Mothers deserved everything good in this world as they were responsible for raising the next generation who would govern the world.

'Yes, a deal. I will promise to ask Luke about my test results, ask about the original paperwork from when I was brought back from Sydney. It must be still kept somewhere here, although I didn't see any of it with my current file.'

Her eyes snapped to his. 'You've been checking your records?'

'I'm not a complete idiot, Kristie, even if I have been acting like one on occasion–'

A small smile touched her face. 'Only on occasion?'

He chuckled. 'Perhaps more than occasionally of late.'

She raised an eyebrow. 'You do know it's against the rules for a patient to go through their records without consulting the staff, Doctor Ryan?'

'Ah, yes, I do, but I'm also part of the staff. So, as I was saying, I did look for my test results, but so far, I haven't been able to locate them. Mary promised to search in the old records room when she had time, but with all the staff shortages lately, she's been too busy. Tomorrow, I'll ask Luke what he knows about them. In return, I'm asking you again, no, I'm begging you, have dinner with me.'

Kristie watched him in silence for so long that he saw everything he now knew he wanted, longed for, slipping away from him. If he lost it, lost her, he would have only himself to blame.

In a quiet voice, Kristie said, 'Yes.'

'Yes?' He couldn't believe she meant what he thought.

'Yes, I'll go to the pub with you. To talk, nothing more.'

Alex nodded his head and watched as, once again, she scurried out of his room. He punched the air with his fist. Yes, he thought, yes. This time he wouldn't make the same mistakes. No matter who the father of Kristie's baby was, he longed for another chance with her.

He wanted another chance at happiness.

13

The historic North Gregory pub was a relic of bygone days, a hotel modernized just enough to make the food amazing while keeping the service old fashioned and friendly. Alex had secured them a table in the corner so they could hear themselves talk over the country music blaring from the jukebox. They'd eaten typical country pub fare. Enormous steaks with lashings of side dishes were followed by homemade cheesecake, all of which Kristie had devoured at an awe-inspiring rate.

Alex leaned back in his chair and laughed.

'What?' Kristie demanded, dragging her gaze upwards from her plate where not even a crumb of cheesecake remained.

He shook his head but didn't bother hiding his amusement. 'I was just wondering if you wanted to lick up that last drop of cream before I ordered you another desert.'

Kristie glanced around to see if anyone else had been watching her. 'Am I making a pig of myself?'

'Not at all. I'm happy to see that your appetite is back. I was worried you weren't eating enough with all these mornings of being sick.'

He leaned his arms on the table and stared as her tongue darted out to lick her lips. She looked like a contented piglet, rubbing her full belly and smacking her lips. Monica's obsession with her figure had meant that every choice was agonized over and dining out lost any appeal and Eliza's strict eating regime allowed no room for indulgences.

Kristie tackled her meal as if she hadn't eaten for days, which relieved his anxiety over whether her morning sickness was continuing into evenings. In deference to her pregnancy, she drank juice as he sipped on a cold beer and watched. In truth, he hadn't been able to drag his eyes off her all night. The sense of rightness he'd discovered in her company in Brisbane had returned with a vengeance.

'I've missed this,' he said, indicating the two of them sitting over their meal.

'Me too.'

She'd been a little preoccupied all night, although he couldn't quite put his finger on what troubled her. He didn't think it was him exactly. Their conversation was stimulating as he tried to keep pace with Kristie's mind leap-frogging through numerous topics. No one could ever call dining with Kristie dull, or peaceful, as her boundless energy made her enter every discussion as if it was a debate on World Peace. Plus, he enjoyed arguing with her. Her eyes flashed and her hair flew in every direction, while her madly waving hands upended a glass or sent cutlery spinning to the floor.

In their second week together, he'd called her a klutz and in typical Kristie fashion, she'd agreed wholeheartedly with him, announcing it was one of her multitude of flaws. However, he didn't see it as a flaw but part of her unique character. At work, she displayed such brisk efficiency that her co-workers were a little intimidated by her. In her personal life, she reverted to an adorable klutz who tripped over nothing and dropped everything.

During dinner, she'd dropped her serviette three times and had barely noticed when he'd bent to retrieve it each time. She'd been too engrossed in telling him her ideas for involving the high school's teenagers in a hospital visiting program where they adopted a long term patient to visit and assist.

Loud voices at a neighboring table interrupted their conversation. Alex saw that Shorty Peterson and his two long time buddies from the shearing shed were drunk enough to become their usual nuisance. The threesome often spent a night in the lockup and the police sergeant had warned them that the next time they caused trouble, they'd earn a much stiffer sentencing.

Shorty's strident voice carried to their table, and probably to every other table in the pub as he pointed at Kristie. 'Look at 'er sitting over there without a worry in the world.'

Beside him, Harry piped up. 'She'll have enough worry soon when word gets out she's pregnant. Her belly will be too big for work at the hospital. Then where'll she be?'

Johnny, the third and roughest member of the gang added, 'Out on 'er big bum, That's where. Mind you, with them tits, she'd get another sorta job any day, if you get me meanin'.'

By the loud laughter from his two mates, they understood his inference only too well. Anger flooded Alex and he shoved back his chair.

Kristie reached over and laid her hand on his arm. She gave him an imploring look. 'Alex, leave it alone. Please. They're drunk.'

But no man could ignore it. It was insulting. No woman would be subjected to that sort of rudeness in his town. With a small smile for Kristie, he removed her hand and stood. As he walked past her chair, he patted her shoulder in a gesture of reassurance. He strode over to the other table, placed his hands on the laminate surface and leaned down close to Shorty.

'You guys are drunk. Why don't you go home and sleep it off before you say anything else you'll regret.'

'Hey, Alex Ryan, me old mate.' Shorty slapped Alex's arm. 'me and the boys don't mean no harm. Just having a little fun talk about your playmate. Story around town is that she's preggers so we was just wonderin' what she'll be doing next for a job. And who she'll be doing it with.'

Johnny watched Kristie's embarrassment with a huge grin on his beaten up face. The scars on his body were a testament to the fact that he never backed down from a fight and he was drunk enough to want to stir up a little action at the pub.

'You better look out, Alex. Good looking guy, fancy doctor, plenty of money. City girl like her'll be after you like a rocket.'

Alex's fist clenched at his sides as he struggled to control his building anger.

Johnny rattled on, oblivious to the danger he was in. 'Maybe even try to claim the kid's yours.'

Goaded beyond rational thinking, Alex announced in a voice that was equally as loud as Johnny's,

'The baby is mine and I do claim it.'

The noise level in the room had dropped away while people listened in to the loud exchange between the four men. After Alex's declaration, the silence became so absolute, you could have heard a pin drop.

Shorty was taken aback enough to stutter an apology for their blunder. 'Jeezus. Sorry mate. We didn't know.' He slapped Alex's arm and wobbled to his feet to stretch out his hand to shake Alex's. 'Good on ya, mate. Didn't know you had it in you.'

Harry did the same. 'Sorry, Alex, but we thought, that is, your stepmother always said...'

The fury in Alex's glare stopped Harry from saying any more but Johnny wobbled drunkenly to his feet. With his large shearer's hand, he slapped Alex on the back, hard enough to knock him off balance.

'Never thought to see the day,' Johnny announced. 'A hoity-toity Ryan taken in by some knocked up girl with a sob story. Better send her off quick, mate. Before she gets them greedy mitts on ya money.'

Alex's arm flexed to swing at Johnny's grinning face but before he could land one, somebody grabbed him from behind and spun him away. Sergeant Tony Baker was a powerfully built man but it took all his strength to control a struggling Alex.

'Whoa, whoa, mate. These idiots aren't worth it. Better go and see to Kristie. She didn't look too good when she ran past me.'

With a nod to the hotel owner who'd phoned for reinforcements the moment he saw Shorty stir up trouble, Alex raced after Kristie. The publican and the police were experts in dealing with the town's biggest nuisances and from the horrified gasps from other diners at Johnny's words, there would be plenty of reinforcements to back them up.

The town wasn't large enough for Kristie to hide. Alex spotted Kristie turning towards the hospital staff quarters and he started running after her, calling out as he ran, 'Kristie, wait.'

She ignored him and quickened her pace. Even from this distance, he could tell she was crying as sobs wrenched her shoulders as she tried to hurry away. Alex's fitness level was still below par and although he sprinted after her, she gained ground. Out of breath, he stopped and bent, hands to his knees and gasped air into his aching lungs.

A hand ran down his spine and a face pressed close beside his. 'You idiot,' Kristie berated him. 'For a doctor, you do some really stupid things.' She hiccoughed and swiped at her wet face, brushing away tears. 'You aren't supposed to be running down streets. You need another week with no stress on your cardiac system after such big doses of antivenom.'

When he straightened, she placed her fingers over the pulse point at his wrist and checked her watch by the streetlight, counting silently.

Amazed, he gulped air and tried to speak. 'You...you came back. Just to check...on me.'

Taking his arm, she guided him to the tourist bench on the side of the footpath. 'Sit there and don't talk until you can breathe again.' For the next sixty seconds, he did what she ordered and concentrated on getting his breathing and pulse rate under control and his thoughts in order.

She was reciting facts, as if straight from a book. 'Brown snake venom contains potent presynaptic neurotoxins that cause paralysis or muscle weakness. A victim should not overtax their system with extreme bursts of physical activity.'

'You've been reading up on me,' he said, unable to hide his wide grin at the idea that she'd been studying all the side effects of snake venom. 'You care.'

'Ha! Of course I care. I don't want you back in my hospital with a relapse.'

He took her hand and held it for a long moment before speaking, not wanting to pull away and run while he made another endeavor, probably another blundering attempt, at getting closer to understanding her feelings. For a doctor with a normally compassionate bedside manner and a reputation as being ultra-sensitive to people's emotional states, he always seemed to make colossal mistakes with her. Always seemed to get off on the wrong foot lately.

'I saw the look on your face before you ran out of the pub. You were angry with me when I told everyone in the pub that the baby was mine.'

'Of course I was angry. You don't even believe what you told them.'

'So why did you come back?'

Rolling her eyes in disgust she declared, 'I couldn't let you collapse on the street.' She looked down and smirked. 'Not next to the dinosaur's feet. People will think you're as old as them. They'll cart you off to the museum.'

A small smile tugged at his lips. She was referring to the large green feet supporting the bench where he now sat. In honor of Eliot, a dinosaur whose skeleton was found on a local property, the town council had gone dinosaur crazy. Seats had dinosaur feet and rubbish tins were prehistoric replicas. Tourists loved it and the town reveled in an economic boom equivalent to times when the country's finances rode on the sheep's back.

'They'd think the truth,' he responded with a heartfelt groan. 'That I'm too old, and not enough of a man, to be a father. To make you pregnant.'

She bristled at his reference to his fertility problems and their argument over her baby's paternity. 'None of that is true.'

'Shorty and the others made it clear they've heard about my

virility problems. Eliza loves to rub it in by telling everyone she meets how pathetic her stepson is.' He gave a bitter laugh. 'After swearing them to secrecy, of course.'

Kristie's eyes narrowed and her face flashed with annoyance. 'It's past time you pulled yourself out of your self-pity party and stood up to Eliza.'

'Christ, you don't pull any punches, do you?'

'Alex, Eliza is wrong.'

'Wrong about what?'

'You look, and act, like the extremely virile thirty-four year old you are. I should know. I've had firsthand experience and she hasn't.'

After dumbfounding him with this revelation, Kristie's face turned a brilliant shade of red. She spun away, kicking a stone up and down the footpath and feigning fascination with a country street totally devoid of nighttime traffic. The only sounds of humanity wafted down from the pub. Alex shuddered at the thought of the bar gossip being bandied about he and Kristie and that by morning, the whole town would know of their relationship.

Two weeks ago, he'd tried to forget he'd ever met Kristie Donaldson. Yet now he wanted, no, he needed her to obsess about him in the same disturbing way she haunted his every waking moment. In that instant, their future crystallised in his mind. Having her, and now her baby, in his life had become as vital as breathing and he was arrogantly confident he could persuade Kristie to accept his resolution. What choice did she have? Sooner or later, if the baby's father didn't step forward, Kristie would see that his impromptu decision in the pub to declare himself a substitute father made a lot of sense.

Right now though, he wasn't about to let Kristie off the hook without enjoying a moment of he-man chest beating. He leaned back on the cartoon character seat and smirked. It made him happy that first, she was worried enough about his health to run back to check on him, and second, she still harbored bedroom type thoughts about him.

'So, you think I'm virile, do you?' he teased. 'Extremely virile?'

She didn't answer but halted her pacing to stop in front of him.

'About tonight, Alex. I want you to forget it. Everything. Everything that happened. I have.'

Her abrupt change of conversation confused him. He frowned. 'Which bit exactly have you forgotten?'

'What you said,' she spat out. 'At the pub.'

His deliberately blank look was designed to raise her ire and he enjoyed it, taking perverse delight in making her spell it out, explain herself in full. 'Which bit?'

Her gaze narrowed on him as she tried to decipher if he was serious or playing games. 'The part where you told the whole room that the baby...' Her hands came up to cover her stomach. She sucked in a deep breath. 'You said the baby was yours.'

'You didn't like me saying that?'

'I did. I loved it.' She glanced down at her abdomen and murmured, 'I just wanted you to want this baby as much as I do.'

'But you didn't like me lying to everyone?'

'See! That's what I mean.' Her head flew up and she stepped closer between his legs. With an angry look, she poked a finger in his chest and yelled in his face, 'You think it's a lie, despite me telling you the baby is yours.'

Alex shook his head, bewildered that she clung to that story when all the evidence indicated otherwise, yet Kristie believed it to be true. His mind reeled. 'It doesn't matter if the baby isn't mine by blood. The real father doesn't seem to be around to claim it, so I will.'

'That's crazy! You're crazy.'

'No, I'm not. Just listen for a minute, Kristie.' He grasped her hand to prevent her from moving, pulling her down to sit beside him on the ridiculous green feet. 'It makes sense.'

'To whom?'

'To me. And if you think about it, to you. It's the sensible solution. If you have no intention of marrying any other man, then why not marry me?'

'Why would you want that when you believe this baby belongs to another man?'

'Because I can't have a child of my own. I need an heir for

Undulla. I'll officially adopt the baby after we're married. It'll be brought up as a Ryan. Your baby will have all the advantages you can't afford to give it by yourself.'

For a minute Kristie didn't speak but when she did, the sadness in her voice tore at his heart. 'Thank you for your kind offer, Doctor Ryan,' she said with stiff formality and rose slowly to her feet. 'But I could never marry a man who doesn't trust me.'

'Then what will you do?' He kept hold of her hand, not wanting her to leave it like this, nothing settled and his heart aching. 'Shorty's right. Once the hospital board discovers you're pregnant, they're not likely to offer you a full time position.'

'I'll figure something else out. For me, and our baby, but while I'm here, can you please just leave me alone.'

Dumbfounded, Alex remained motionless, alone on the seat, as Kristie tugged away from him and jogged across the deserted street towards the hospital. That entire conversation had gone horribly wrong. He'd offered her a future with him, a genuine offer of help, yet she'd tossed it back in his face. For Kristie, his wealth or his status didn't matter. An offer of marriage from him wasn't enough. He needed to prove himself to her as a man, and as a father to her baby. For years he'd had women throw themselves at him because of who he was, what he owned. Yet, the one woman he really wanted in his life had turned her back on him. Spurned his offer as if it was contaminated, or as if he was diseased and he was at a loss to know what to do next.

That night, he lay propped up in bed and replayed the conversation over and over in his mind for hours. Kristie truly believed he was the man who had impregnated her, no one else, yet he'd stuck to his highhanded assumption that he was right. He'd shown he didn't trust in her enough to take even the simplest of steps to investigate the facts. His medical training ought to have taught him there could be a slim chance. A very slim chance.

However, if Eliza had been completely honest with him, it would take a miracle. But since when did he believe everything his stepmother said. Hadn't she proved to be capable of anything to manipulate people to do her bidding. Perhaps he was just another pawn in her chess game of life. Tomorrow he would find out. He owed that much to Kristie.

Early the next morning, Alex hunched in the passenger seat of his plane being flown to Emerald by his foreman, Rusty. Piloting himself wasn't a good idea this week. He and Luke had studied the warnings about reactions to antivenom and as this was his second time bitten, his risk of anaphylactic shock was far greater. The chances of side effects this long after the two doses were slim but risking it would be stupid.

Alex refused to have this particular test done at Dinosaur Valley hospital or the gossip mill would have it spread all over town in an hour, and there were certain people that he didn't want to know just yet, one being his stepmother and the other Luke. His mate, Luke, who'd been in charge of all his previous test results. It disgusted him to even harbor the slightest suspicion against either one of them, but he prided himself on being an intelligent man. A man who made logical decisions and followed rational paths of investigation. He shook his head to clear his wandering thoughts.

Today's excursion may prove a wild goose chase but if there was the slightest possibility he'd been misled, no, more than misled. Lied to, by someone close to him, he needed to discover it, and do it soon, before anyone else got hurt, especially Kristie. He'd hurt her already by believing she was the one telling lies. If he discovered he'd wronged her, he made a silent vow to spend the rest of his life making it up to her. If he got the chance.

At Emerald hospital he was unknown, plus it serviced the young male population who worked on the mines so hospital staff were more accustomed to sperm testing. Surely they'd provide the customary private room, a specimen jar and a Playboy magazine or two. Although allowing his thoughts to wander where they went each and every night lately, to the remembered pleasures of having Kristie in his bed, moaning under him in ecstasy, would be enough to fill his cup in a short time.

Having repeat test results would prove to her that he was serious about answering all her concerns. It would also prove to himself whether Eliza had lied to him or not. Or if Luke had betrayed him. Being a doctor did nothing to alleviate his embarrassment at having to go through this, but the next time he asked Kristie to marry him, he intended it to be a legitimate proposal. Not a spur of the moment question.

14

Kristie sat behind her desk struggling with tedious paperwork although her wits weren't centered on staff rosters, or hospital budgets. For the fiftieth time, her gaze strayed to the car park where she'd become accustomed to seeing Alex's four wheel drive parked.

For a week he'd been an inpatient and then he'd followed Luke's orders and stayed in town at the hotel for four days. During those eleven days he'd come and gone often, attending hospital meetings and assisting Luke with his heavy load of clinic appointments. From staff room gossip, Kristie knew that Alex had done his internship rotations at nearby regional hospitals and still often helped out, free of charge, at all their clinics.

At a delivery room demonstration two days ago, twenty pregnant women with out of control hormones had drooled over Luke and Alex, making a joke out of it with their husbands in the room. It wasn't often that two of the most gorgeous specimens of manhood on the planet dropped into isolated outback towns to help horny women twist into positions best suited to a bedroom.

Worst of all, each time Kristie had crouched beside an expectant couple to give instructions, she'd bumped into Alex or Luke. Luke had created a game out of how many times he could bump her rear end but she'd been terrified that Alex would bump into her too, or rub against her over sensitized body. If that had happened, her own raging hormones may have driven her to throw Alex to an exercise mat for a demonstration of what repressed lust could do to a normally sane person.

Yesterday, Alex and his truck hadn't appeared until afternoon. So she'd spent the morning staring out the window like a love sick teenager watching for her adolescent crush to drive past. Today, her agitation had escalated to the point where if Alex so much as glanced sideways at her, she'd pounce and drag him into her office and lock the door.

Maxine and the other staff were bound to notice her pathetic behavior and pass comments because their curiosity over her relationship with Alex increased every day. Although, their gentle understanding of her surprise condition had nearly reduced her to tears three times this week already. She was turning into a complete watering pot and Alex had caught her at it yesterday. He'd nodded knowingly and muttered doctor type things about pregnancy hormones, which had only made her cry harder.

Despite being an intelligent nurse who recognized all the medical reasons for her erratic behavior, Alex's clinical diagnosis angered her. Her feminine side cried out for him to scoop her up and rush her to the nearest bed, not pacify her like a fretful child. When faced with Alex's country gentleman proposal of marriage to a woman in trouble, she'd reciprocated with a ladylike and necessary refusal. Now, in utter frustration, she bemoaned her stupidity for not grabbing hold of him and not letting go until they stood before a minister in church.

In her more rational moments, she acknowledged that a marriage based on mistrust and conflicting motives would never suffice. Nor should it be enough for Alex. Their connection was too intense for either of them to settle for half a marriage. Her feelings for him were too strong to settle for less than a union based on love, not necessity.

A loud knock was a welcome interruption to her turbulent thoughts yet, even as she called for her visitor to enter, part of her hoped that it was Alex. She yearned for his six feet something, sex in jeans and boots body to appear around her door and gaze at her with hunger.

Sergeant Tony Brooks certainly fulfilled part of her fantasy as he was tall and lanky and according to several single girls in town, also sexy. The sergeant's gaze even held a hint of hunger as he looked her over and sauntered closer. Disappointment deflated Kristie, but she regrouped enough to infuse her voice with some enthusiasm.

'Tony, hi. I hope you're here to cheer me up. Tell me you've found my ghostly ex-patient.'

When he chuckled, she smiled in appreciation as a gorgeous dimple emerged from each tanned cheek. Yep, she could definitely see why the girls in town ogled him.

'Good news.' He flashed her a film star grin hot enough to melt most woman's heart, but it had no effect on her at all. 'We have a promising lead on your disappearing corpse. We learned from neighbors that the hearse left the council yard at six o'clock in the morning. Twenty minutes later, it was seen being driven away from the hospital by a man wearing dark glasses and a black cloak and talking on a mobile phone.'

'Great. We just need to search every house in town for someone who looks like he stepped out of the Matrix. Our own personal Neo in outback Australia.'

Perched on the corner of her desk, Tony roared with laughter. 'I can just see this town as a Sci Fi movie set. But don't worry because we'll soon catch this superhero. You see, they needed the hearse because they also stole a funeral casket from the council storeroom. The best casket they keep. Purple velvet lining, brass handles, the whole works.'

'Someone wants to bury Wilhelm in style then, but why not just wait until after the autopsy?' As soon she voiced her query understanding dawned. 'Ah, of course.'

'Yep. Somebody,' he said, raising his brows in emphasis, 'is afraid of the autopsy results. Which means that all fingers point to someone in the family. As does stealing the best casket in town.'

'Have you found the hearse?'

Tony gave her a smug smile as he nodded. 'Yep. It was abandoned just outside town a couple of hours after it was taken.'

'I guess it's too much to hope that the casket was in it. Or Wilhelm.'

'Afraid not, but we're searching the Schmidt's properties now. We're pretty certain we'll find Wilhelm in one of the cold rooms they use for their meat business.'

Kristie shuddered. 'Ooooh, gross. If people find out, they'll boycott the butcher shop this week.'

'It's a shame really because the Schmidt family are nice people. If they've done this, they must have a very good reason.'

Tony's long khaki covered legs stretched out towards her so one regulation police boot nudged her hospital lace up shoe. The temperature in the room climbed. Heat flooded her face as she picked up more than a hint of male interest in his pacific blue eyes. Oh, my goodness. She wanted hunger and was getting hunger. Just not from the right man.

To put some distance between them, she straightened in her chair and tucked her feet under, but Tony's knowing eyes followed every move. He gave a teasing grin at her subtle attempt to move away and inched closer along the edge of her desk.

'Kristie, I came in person to tell you that little snippet of information, because I wanted to ask you to have dinner with me.'

'She's pregnant.'

The thunderous voice made she and Tony jump with fright, pull back from each other and gape at the doorway. Alex leaned on her office wall in a relaxed cross-legged stance, however, his shoulders were bunched under his double-pocket workman's shirt.

Tony stood in a languid movement but didn't move away from behind Kristie's desk. 'Alex, we didn't hear you come in.'

'Obviously.'

Kristie noted the antagonism flash between the two men and knew they'd played this scene before. Alex's gaze narrowed as he glanced between she and Tony, assessing the situation. He didn't look happy.

She waved a hand between them. 'You two are obviously acquainted.'

Alex answered, 'Yes, but not in a good way. We played footie together as kids.'

Tony, undeterred by Alex's attitude, met his glare with an even wider grin. 'Alex and I have always competed over something.' He laid a hand on Kristie's shoulder and she was certain he only did it to irritate Alex. 'Growing up, we fought over football, school, women.'

'Okay, Tony. You've delivered your official message. Now you can leave.'

Tony ignored him and bent towards Kristie to ask, 'So, about dinner, will eight be okay?' He leaned in even closer and dropped his voice to a seductive invitation. 'It would be my pleasure to show you the sights of Winton.'

Before Kristie had a chance to voice her polite refusal, Alex strode towards Tony. He stood with his hands on his hips and feet planted wide apart and snapped, 'There are no sights to see in Winton.'

Undaunted, Tony moved to stand face to face with Alex and declare, 'There are at my place.'

Kristie pushed up out of her chair and tried to step around her desk and between the two glaring men. 'Would you two stop it? You're being ridiculous.'

Giving her an apologetic look, Alex took Tony by the elbow and led him to the door and into the corridor. Left standing alone in her office, Kristie shook her head in disbelief at the foolishness of the male species. These two alpha males were so busy beating their chests in competition over a woman, her, that they forgot she could still hear them. And see them.

'Tony.' Alex's voice was loud and angry. 'I'm warning you to stop trying to hit on Kristie. Besides, she works hard and needs to rest at night.'

'I think we should let the lovely lady decide for herself if she is up to eating with me.'

Irritation was evident in every spasm of Alex's body as he said again, 'I've already told you, Kristie's pregnant.'

'Pregnant ladies need to eat dinner. And gossip says you've relinquished any prior claim you had on our gorgeous Director of Nursing. So, I can ask her out without stepping on your toes.'

'I have not relinquished anything where Kristie is concerned.'

'Ah, so you're claiming to be the father of her baby, are you?'

Kristie held her breath waiting for Alex's answer but his silence spoke volumes. He was still denying her and her child. Tears threatened but she forced them back, straightened her spine, and stepped out to face the two men. 'Both of you, leave now,' she yelled, pointing to the car park. 'I won't listen to you fight over me like dogs with a bone. And I'm not going to be part of your ongoing rivalry to prove who is top dog in town.'

Both men looked embarrassed. Alex reached out to her but she quickly stepped back inside her office and slammed the door, turning the lock. Leaning against the wood, she tried to get herself under control. If it wasn't so serious, it would be comical. Two ridiculously handsome men fighting over a pregnant woman. So why was she crying, not laughing?

Alex's angry voice reverberated through the wood as he berated Tony, 'Now look what you've done.'

'Me? I just asked her out for dinner. It's you she's angry at,' Tony said, his voice fading as he walked away. 'If you really want to keep Kristie, you're going to have to work a lot harder to make her want to stay.'

She didn't unlock the door until she thought they'd left, putting her head down and trying to concentrate on paperwork. Unfortunately, the bout of tears came no matter how hard she fought them back. But she'd never hidden from trouble before and she wasn't about to start now. If Alex didn't want them, she and her baby would still be a family. Other towns had hospitals where she could work and after living in the outback, Kristie knew she didn't want to live anywhere else. A town like this one, with down to earth people who cared, was where she wanted her son or daughter to be born. Out here, kids grew up strong and capable, safe and loved.

The thought made her smile and she gave her stomach a reverent pat before stepping out into the corridor. Ouch! She tripped over a pair of long legs, only this time they were covered in worn denim, not khaki. Alex had stretched out on the floor to wait for Kristie to open her door and each heart-wrenching sob he'd heard had twisted his gut.

He'd done this to her, made her cry, again, and he didn't want to do it to her anymore. He remembered her being so happy in Brisbane, laughing and playful as they'd romped through their days together and he wanted that Kristie back again.

Lost in thought, he didn't hear the door opening. When she fell over his legs, he'd tried to catch her but then the feel of her landing on him had robbed him of coherent thought. A soft armful of woman dropped onto his lap. Going with the sensation, he held her against him and breathed deeply. She was soft all over, so womanly and lush that he wanted to bury himself in her and never come up for air, but she pushed off him and stood.

Her eyes were red rimmed from crying and he felt like the biggest heel who ever walked the planet as he jumped to his feet and took her hands in his. He didn't remember Monica ever allowing tears to smudge her makeup and Eliza was far too controlled to allow anyone to view her in a moment of human frailty. By contrast, Kristie never feared showing emotion, be it good or bad. She'd melted watching Grace at the plane, caring for her injured husband with so much love on her face. The fretful children and the dribbling babies Kristie constantly carried on her hip made her smile with joy.

'Kristie, I don't care who the father is.'

'That's not what you said before, Alex. You didn't believe me when I told you the baby is yours and every chance you get, you ask me who the father is.'

'I'm sorry. I've been stupid. Give me another chance, please?'

She was silent for a few moments before asking, 'What do you want from me, Alex?'

'I want you to marry me. I want the baby to be born a Ryan.'

'And I've already said I won't marry a man who doesn't believe in me.'

Inwardly he groaned. He'd ruined everything with his insistence on dictating to her, or interrogating her, at every opportunity. 'Then at least come to Undulla and spend the weekend with me. We can talk, without the whole town watching us.'

She gave a short laugh. 'That's actually very tempting. The staff are being wonderful but they're smothering me with their concern. I'm getting worn out with everyone here watching every move I make. Every morning when I have morning sickness, they cluck over me like a group of mother hens.'

He smiled at the image, pleased that his friends were taking care of her. 'They mean well.'

'I know.'

'And we could go and visit Daniel Mitchell.' When Kristie's eyes lit up in excitement, Alex pushed his advantage. 'He did invite you to see the dinosaur digs.'

The ends of her mouth tipped up in a tiny glimmer of a smile. 'I'd really love that.'

He felt elated. She was going to come to his home. Then he noticed her frown. Uh, oh.

'But what about Eliza? She won't want me there.'

His enthusiasm deflated a little but he was determined to get Kristie alone so they could talk. Or anything else that might eventuate on a moonlit night in the bush. 'Eliza's leaving. Going away for a week. We'll have the place to ourselves. I really want a chance to show you around. I want you to think about living at Undulla with me.'

'I don't know if it's a good idea for us to be alone again for the whole weekend. Remember what happened in the ambulance?'

'Tommy's wife, Peg, is our housekeeper so if it makes you feel better, I'll arrange for her to be there. Please, just come.'

Nothing. She didn't answer and he had no right to pressure her further when she was in such a vulnerable state. He closed his eyes as he prepared himself to forgo his hopes that she'd forgive him. His throat moved convulsively as he tried to summon the words to say goodbye.

When she finally spoke, it was a whispered word. 'Yes.'

His eyes popped open. 'Yes?' When she nodded, he heaved out a relieved grunt. 'Thank you. I'll come and collect you after you finish work on Friday.'

'No, I'd rather drive myself. That way I can leave if it's uncomfortable for either of us.'

He fought to stay calm and not demand she allow him to take care of her, and her baby. After all, it was her independent attitude that he'd first admired about her so he had no right to criticize it now.

'Okay. Until Friday then. I'm looking forward to it.' Alex turned and left before he gave in to his urge to take her in his arms again and comfort her. Friday seemed a long time away.

In his office at Undulla later that day, Alex caught sight of his stepmother hovering in the doorway and scowling at him. He put down the box of files he'd been searching through.

'Yes, Eliza. Was there something you wanted?'

Even as he asked he was fairly sure what was upsetting her, as he knew she'd just finished a phone call with one of her cronies in town. Dinosaur Valley's gossip mill was always efficient and Kristie was quite correct in assuming his stepmother wouldn't be pleased that he'd invited her to Undulla. Nevertheless, it was way past time that he decided about his own future instead of bending over backwards to please everyone else and in doing so, neglected what made him happy.

Kristie was also correct that he missed practicing full time medicine like a nagging ache in his chest. He'd wanted to be a doctor his whole life and putting it on the back burner for so many months didn't sit well. In fact, it was making him totally miserable. In the last two weeks, his eyes had opened to so many things in his life that he needed to change. And the most important was his attitude towards Kristie. If he wanted to keep her with him, he needed to do something in a hurry or she'd leave Dinosaur Valley and their relationship would be finished, forever.

Eliza marched into the room and leaned on his desk, manicured nails drumming on the rosewood and her perfectly made up face glaring at him. 'You cannot be serious. How dare you invite a person like her into my home?'

'Need I remind you, Eliza, that this house actually still belongs to me. And the way things are looking, it may remain mine.'

Her eyes widened with horror. 'What about Ben? He's expecting you to sign Undulla over to him as soon as he's finished his Agricultural Degree.'

'No, Eliza, Ben isn't expecting it. You are. I've never discussed the possibility with Ben. And depending on Kristie's answer, I may never do it.'

'What answer?'

Like a lovesick idiot, he smiled when he thought about her answer and what it would mean if she said yes. Convincing her that it was best for her baby was becoming his obsession. The idea that she might refuse his offer gnawed like a cancer but he arrogantly refused to acknowledge it.

'I've asked Kristie to marry me.'

'Marry you! How dare you.' For the first time in many months, Eliza's publicly hidden but privately fiery temper snapped to the forefront. Since his accident, Alex had conceded to her demands on a daily basis simply to maintain peace in the household. It was his way of doing penance to his father for not returning to Undulla when he was still alive. Before, he'd seen no reason to fight. Now, he had something to fight for. Or someone.

'You will not give some unknown girl from the city the Ryan name. What about her baby? You know it isn't yours.'

'Do I, Eliza? Actually, I wanted to ask you about that. I've searched through the paperwork from my accident. I found dozens of blood results and a box of notes on physiotherapy and other treatments. There are dates and times from my ambulance transfer from the hospital in Brisbane to Dinosaur Valley. No results for any sperm test. Why is that?'

Emotions raced across her face in such rapid succession that Alex couldn't be sure, but he thought one was guilt. His already awakened suspicions heightened. However, when she answered she appeared calm and in control once more. After first Maxine and then Kristie planted the seeds of doubt in his mind, he'd become suspicious that someone was lying to him. But was he now accusing innocent people of committing crimes in order to justify his belief in Kristie?

His naiveté in believing Eliza's version of events after his accident now appalled him. As a doctor he had enough knowledge and intelligence to have stayed on top of it all. In his own defense, the combination of pain and depression from his injuries, the death of his friend and Monica's desertion had drained his energy. Eliza's outlook and assuming command had felt like a blessing, yet in hindsight, it could be construed as an over-ambitious intrusion into his life.

'After your accident, we were all so distraught.' She fluttered her hands and gave a helpless look although this time Alex remained skeptical. 'Things got misplaced. I'm sure that if you cannot locate something, it's simply been misfiled.'

'But now I can think about it all in a more rational frame of mind, Eliza, a sperm count is a really strange test to do on a patient who is barely coherent and recovering from multiple injuries. It wouldn't have been the normal thing to do at all.'

'You didn't just have a fractured leg, Alex, you had internal damage. Your legs, your whole ... whole area.' She did a fluttery wave of her hand again in the direction of his lower body. 'Everything was swollen. There was so much bruising that at first they thought they'd need to remove your spleen. They did all sorts of investigations.'

'So, who gave permission for the tests?'

'You did of course.'

'Me?' He shook his head in confusion. 'I thought I was unconscious for the first four days. And not coherent for another week after that. Isn't that what you told me?'

Eliza jumped up from the other chair where she had barely

seated herself and turned towards the door. 'I really can't remember such trivial matters, Alex.'

'Trivial?' He leapt to his feet and strode out from behind his desk. 'It's hardly trivial for me. It affects my entire life, my entire future. If I can't father a child, it would be unfair of me to offer marriage to a woman.'

Spinning back to glare at him, she said, 'Then you should send Ms. Donaldson away from town immediately.'

'Kristie's situation is different. She's already pregnant. And there is always a chance that it could be mine.'

'Rubbish, Alex. That's just wishful thinking.'

'The chance is a slim one, I know. But I'm willing to take the risk if it means I can have a family.'

'You already have a family.' Eliza's face tightened in anger. 'Ben and Amanda, and me. Your father will turn over in his grave if you allow that nurse's child to become any part of Undulla. The baby will never be a legitimate Ryan.'

'But then, neither are Ben or Amanda.' Alex regretted the stark harshness of his words when shock paled his stepmother's face to an unbecoming white, which even the layer of expensive make up couldn't conceal.

'That is a despicable thing to say about your brother and sister. Your father always intended formally adopting them both.'

Something about that had always nagged at him. 'Yes, so why did that never happen?'

Flustered, Eliza snapped her answer at him, leaving him in no doubt that he'd touched a raw nerve. 'Your father simply ran out of time. Now it's your duty to rectify that terrible omission.'

Before Alex could say anything to dispute her assumption that it was his responsibility to rectify his father's lapses, she turned and fled the room. Ten minutes later, he saw Rusty driving Eliza to the landing strip and a half hour after that, he heard their plane take off. Eliza was attending a friend's party on the coast but her hurry to avoid finishing the conversation they'd been having, left him even more puzzled. And more than a little concerned.

There'd been plenty of time for his father to have started the formalities of adopting of his step siblings and having their names changed to Ryan, if that had been his intent. Yet, he'd never done it. So now, Alex wondered why. And he knew exactly who to ask for those answers. Mary Klein knew every crumb of the town's intricate family history for the last forty years.

He picked up the phone and dialed. Answers were needed and he was determined to get them. And quickly, before he lost another person he loved.

15

Friday became the longest day Alex had ever spent. He fretted that Kristie would change her mind and not come for the weekend. Each day away from her was getting harder to bear. She lightened up his life, lifted him from his worries, yet despite that, her pregnancy haunted him day and night. As a doctor, and her friend, he felt responsible for her health and that of her baby.

The strong protective instinct he felt was nothing new for him. Colleagues teased him from his first years as an intern that he was too much of a soft touch to become a hard-nosed surgeon. Becoming a pediatrician was a natural step for a doctor whose soft-hearted approach made it easier to deal with children than spend hours standing over an operating table in silence.

When her old car rattled over the cattle grid at six o'clock, he was so relieved to see her that he rushed outside to greet her. Giving her no chance to object, he scooped her up and swung her around, hugging her as he did so, until she objected with a giggling laugh.

'Alex, enough. I'm pleased you're so eager to see me but you're going to turn my morning sickness into evening sickness.'

'Oh, I'm sorry. I was just so pleased to see you arrive, to know you hadn't backed out of our arrangement that I forgot.' He collected her bag form the car and took her arm, leading her inside. 'What would you like to do first? Have a rest before I organize dinner? A cup of tea? Whatever would make you most comfortable.'

'You.'

'Me? Me what?'

'You make me most comfortable. And, yes, I'd like a rest. On a bed. A big bed. With you.' She lifted to her toes and kissed him, a touch so sweet that almost melted in a puddle at her feet.

Nevertheless, he was determined to do the right thing this time. He wanted to show her his home and make her feel comfortable here, and welcome enough she'd want to live here. With him.

He swallowed hard. 'Peg is coming to chaperone us later, over dinner. I thought you'd feel more comfortable that way.'

'Well, you'd better ring Peg and tell her she's not needed until breakfast time tomorrow. I'm certain to be starving by then.' She ran a finger in a leisurely fashion down his chest and over his jean's zipper.

There was no way she could miss the bulge in his pants but he left it up to her. 'The way I see it, you have two choices. Continue taunting me and suffer the consequences, the same as in the ambulance. Or save yourself and run, because in another few minutes I'm going to pick you up and carry you off to my bedroom and you won't see daylight before tomorrow's breakfast, that's for sure. Once I have you where I want you, in my bed and spread under me...,' he smirked, ' ... as my love slave—'

'Ha! Uh, uh, other way around,' she teased. 'You can be my sex slave, for the entire weekend. Have you forgotten how horny pregnant women can get in their early months?'

Alex couldn't speak, couldn't rediscover his tongue. Instead, he scooped her up into his arms and strode to the door while trying not to laugh and trip over her silly comments all the way.

'Ooh, you Tarzan and me Jane.' She squeezed his bicep and batted her lashes. 'Hmm! I do love the strong silent type.'

'When I get you inside, you'll discover I'm not that silent. And neither will you be.'

'Oh, my goodness. Now you're skiting.'

He laughed, his full body rumbles brushing her breasts where they lay squashed against his chest and increasing his arousal three-fold. 'Christ! I mightn't survive the whole weekend.'

Looking down at her, he sighed. Almost everything he'd ever wanted was in his arms: a warm bundle of squirming and playful woman who challenged him on so many levels, and a woman carrying inside her womb the miracle of a future birth. This was it! More important than upholding the title of world- renowned surgeon and more fulfilling than cattle holdings, no matter how many thousand acres he owned. Someone to share laughter with, someone to form a family bond around, and a woman with whom he could revel and enjoy and just be himself, especially in the bedroom.

He set her down gently onto her feet on the top step of his home and savored the experience of having a special woman here at last. 'We're perfect together. Stay with me.'

She sucked in a breath and touched his face. 'Let's just enjoy what we have here and now, Alex. If my job isn't renewed because I'm pregnant, I'll have to leave here and find another place to work. Too many complications.'

'But you were the one who came here to me, you wanted to have another try. I know it's been hard for you. Small towns are often not very forgiving of newcomers and their problems. Also, I know the criticism about you being pregnant and unmarried must hurt. But please don't give up on me yet. Give me another chance to put things right, okay?'

She nodded slowly. 'We'll enjoy every moment we have together and see what eventuates in the future. That can be our promise to each other.'

They went to his room and he shut the door, locking out the rest of the world. For now, she was here and she was his. Willingly. Wantonly his. And he'd be an even greater fool if he wasted a single moment. Lovemaking was the way they had always been closest and he'd use that now to bind her tighter to him.

'Your love slave awaits your orders, my darling. What would you have me do?'

She looked him up and down and his muscles tightened in anticipation. Christ, she only had to look at him and he wanted her with such yearning that it made him shake. 'Ah, well I think the first thing any love slave should remember is that you remain unclothed whenever you are in my presence.'

'Of course, my lady. Whatever you desire.'

He threw off his clothing and tossed it away without even bothering to look. His erection rose and bobbed proudly as if it sensed the appearance of its mate and, like a diving rod seeking water, was searching for her. Moving towards her centre so he could join them, fill her, ease his bleak soul.

'Do you,' he said, swallowing hard, 'do you want me to undress you now, Your Highness?'

She smiled, a seductive siren's smile that had the blood rushing hotly to his groin. 'You may do that, my slave, for I am fatigued. Be sure to pleasure each and every inch of my body as you do so. I have been starved for a man's touch for a very long time. Days, weeks, without the feel of a man's muscled body sliding over me and now, I'm desperate. Love me, Alex. Love me with everything that is in you.'

His hand came out as he stepped forward and tugged her into his arms, too desperate to wait, too wild to even let her finish her fantasy. 'Later,' he murmured in agony. 'Later I'll worship every inch of your pink flesh. But not now. Now I'm too desperate to kiss you,' he dragged a finger up and over her groin. 'Too desperate to be inside you.'

Between them both, they managed to drag her clothing off without tearing it to shreds but it was a close call. He wasn't sure who was now the more desperate. Him, or the woman who stood before him and panting with arousal. Dropping to his knees before her, he used his thumbs to part her and too eager to even stop to survey and admire, he dipped his head. His tongue lashed her from bottom to top and back again, over and over, until her knees where he clasped them wide, shook.

He walked her backward sot the bed and laid her over the edge so his mouth could feast in a free fashion of every glistening exposed inch. They made love in a frantic fashion that first time and then cried out with the same abandon at their climax.

Their next bout of passion was slower but still not orderly or simple or languid. It seemed they were destined to ignite sparks off each other. Each time they came together, too many to count over the next two days, it was an explosion. One that never seemed to subside. When they finally emerged from his bedroom the next day, it was in search of sustenance. He had indeed told Peg not to come to work. In fact, he actually blushed when he told her to not come within a kilometer of the house for the whole weekend. He wanted Kristie to himself and didn't want to share these precious moments.

Peg's response, as had her husband Tommy's was to laugh raucously. Then in all sincerity, they had congratulated Alex on making such a good choice in women. The inference was that he'd made the right choice this time, in comparison to the mess he'd made of his relationship with Monica. Only now did he understand how worried all his friends had been for him when he'd been sucked into the social city whirl and made a series of stupid choices. They'd said nothing. Not one person had uttered criticism to his face over his ridiculous choice of a super model for a wife. As if she was ever going to be happy living on Undulla, especially if he chose to stay in Dinosaur Valley and work permanently.

Kristie had made it clear she'd welcome that choice. Monica had run like the wind as soon as the possibility had been mentioned. How stupid he'd been not to see it but at the time, he'd had Eliza congratulating him for the first time ever on his excellent choice of a wife. Eliza had at first sung Monica's praises but then, upon realizing that a marriage to Monica would keep Alex away from Undulla, and therefore out of reach to give Ben advice, she'd quickly changed her tune.

On Saturday, Alex was determined to show Kristie some of his home, some of the land that belonged to him and all future Ryans. He drove her for hours around boundary fences and over creek beds, some running water, some dry. As he went, he pointed out the good and the bad of living out here.

They stopped at his favorite water hole to picnic and swim, stripping off their dusty clothes with abandon and diving into the deep clear rock pool. Kristie had hesitated for a moment.

'What is it, sweetheart?'

'This is going to sound silly, and I have no right to even ask, but, Alex—'

'Ah! I think I know the question burning a hole in your tongue. The dilemma you are facing before dipping those beautiful toes into my water. The answer is 'No'.' He laughed. 'Can you really imagine that Monica, who loathed getting her hair wet under any circumstances, would have been swimming here with me.' He pulled her into his arms and bent to kiss her. 'No, sweetheart. You're the only person I've been swimming naked with here—' He broke off and started to laugh out aloud.

'What's so funny?'

'I just realized that I told you a lie. You're not the first female to have been swimming naked here with me. When we were younger, and learning about bodies, Maxine and Jenny dared me to strip off one day and dive in here naked.' He snorted. 'Turns out that no one in their boarding house at the school in the city had a photo of a naked boy. So, at thirteen, I became the pin-up model for ten prepubescent girls. My show biz career lasted for all of fifteen minutes.'

'What happened?'

'Teachers happened. Max and Jenny spent most of that term in detention.'

'Did you get punished?'

'No, because you see, in their excitement to photograph my glorious teenage body, they pressed the camera button at the wrong times. The pictures they were hoping to capture and show their friends of a country stud were nothing more than a glimpse of a bare backside with no indication at all who it belonged to.'

She giggled at his story. 'So, you escaped punishment?'

'Yep. To this day the girls have never reported my part in that prank. We were always a bit like the three musketeers, but they knew how much trouble I'd been in if my father ever found out. He would have come down on me like a ton of bricks. And of course, I said nothing because they'd promised me that in exchange for a glimpse of perfection—'

'Ouch!' She'd lightly punched his arm in mock disgust. 'Well at that age, like all teenage boys, I thought my developing physique was awe-inspiring.'

Kristie rolled her eyes and looked so adorable that he had to kiss her again.

'Anyway, my reward never eventuated. One of the girls was so incensed at having to detention all term that she refused my payment. Which was, a complete set of swap cards for that season's winning football team from Melbourne. Thirteen year old girls were a lot more advanced than boys the same age. Where they studied anatomy, boys studied sport.'

'You must have been a handful back then.'

He waggled his eyebrows and pushed his shaft into her hand. 'I'm a handful now.'

She burst out laughing and Alex thought he'd never seen a more wonderful sight. Kristie as a nurse at work took his breath away with her organized and efficient manner. When she was in his bed, she was a vibrant and exciting partner, full of surprises. But here, in this little hidden piece of Nirvana and stripping off her own clothing, she was perfection. A goddess. When he told her that, she laughed but he knew that he'd carry that image of the relaxed side of her to his dying day.

'You're so beautiful,' he murmured.

'And you must need glasses,' she challenged as she scrambled down into the pool and then turned to welcome him with outstretched arms.

H shook his head in denial. She was magnificent and hopefully, for going any other major upheavals in their lives, soon to be his. As he made lazy love to her in an outback lagoon, he thanked God for giving him so much. Not many months ago, he'd thought all the good things had been wrenched away from his grasp.

Now he felt grateful. He knew now that returning to the city wasn't for him anymore. Country life was what he wanted for the next stage in his life, and to practice medicine in the bush and to live his life amongst friends.

And lovers, or one at least, but the most important one. Her, the woman who completed him.

16

Alex watched and waved as Kristie drove away, back to the hospital. He'd wanted to drive her and make sure she was safe, but she'd insisted that she was capable and besides, she didn't want the whole town taking note of their being together. Not yet anyway. She'd begged for more time to get to know the townspeople before the Ryan name became involved. Her argument had been that once people realized that they were seriously a couple, people would treat her differently simply because the Ryan family held sway in the town in so many things.

As her car turned onto the main road and out of sight, he sighed. Already the house echoed with loneliness. Their weekend together had been nothing short of blissful for him, and he hoped her. Kristie's scent lingered on his skin after the number of times they'd made love, and her face filled his vision. He already missed her with an ache to his middle. He rubbed a hand over the place it hurt and then realized it was not only his gut that pained, but his heart.

Each time they parted he felt it as a physical wrench, an ache that as a doctor he was helpless to explain rationally. He only knew that as a man, it hurt. The sooner they fixed the problem and sorted out where their relationship was headed the better for everyone concerned. Ironic, he thought, that he'd been the one doing the running and yet now, when he wanted to get closer to Kristie, she was the one who was unsure. She had begged for more time.

Christ! If only life wasn't so complicated. He was pretty certain that her main reservation stemmed from their now unspoken disagreement over the paternity of her baby. He'd told her it didn't matter to him who the real father was and he'd told her in every way but the direct words that he was in love with her. He always had been and always would be. And this time, he was determined not to mess it up. Not to ruin his only chance at happiness. Which meant either trusting her word and believing the baby was his or that his sperm count had been wrong. Or falsified. He shuddered. That thought was gnawing a hole in his stomach.

If it was true, it had to have been done by one of the people he trusted most and the idea sickened him. He wanted a life with Kristie more than he wanted to ignore unpleasantness, if that was what was coming his way when he unearthed the truth. Someone would be hurt, he knew that, and he was equally determined it wouldn't be Kristie this time. He'd done more than enough damage in that department. In fact, if what he suspected was the truth, then the entire Ryan family had done Kristie a disservice.

When he'd been ill, she'd helped. She'd come running to assist him and form what he gathered now, nobody had taken the time to even thank her for his efforts. He was guilty of that more than the others, yet the niggling doubt remained that someone else had harmed her more. That this whole affair could have been avoided if the truth and nothing but the truth had been disclosed after his accident.

Well, he decided, looking around the empty rooms. No time like the present to solve a mystery. Starting with Eliza's bedroom was a despicable invasion of her privacy, but a necessary one. Still, he'd avoided it as long as he could. He'd already searched the office for any incriminating documents, either about his sperm count testing or about why his father never legally adopted Ben and Amanda. Now he turned out every conceivable hidey hole his father may have used to hide his secrets.

By now, he'd more or less decided that no paperwork on his sperm count existed in this house. If there had indeed been tests carried out, then whoever had been responsible had destroyed any evidence. And if it had been destroyed, that would mean there had been a compelling reason to get rid of them before others saw it.

After two hours of house searching, he was no closer to a solution to the puzzle so the only thing left to do was go through the paperwork he knew Eliza kept in her French writing desk in her room. Damn! He felt like a criminal as he walked into her room and pulled open the desk drawers. Another hour passed and still nothing. He slumped down into the petite chair that matched the feminine desk and dropped his forearms to his knees. Nothing. And now he felt dreadful.

He'd never really warmed to Eliza but he'd spent a lot of year trying to at least not rock the boat with her, not cause waves. Especially when his father had been alive. His visits home had been strained enough with the continued ritual of brow beating Alex into staying on Undulla permanently. The added pressure of him squabbling with Eliza would have been too much to handle for Ben and Amanda, and him. So, in his teen years, he'd elected himself as peacekeeper and it was a role he still played today.

It seemed he was the only buffer of sanity the two kids ever had against the neurosis of their mother. They'd always told him how grateful they were to him for protecting them from so much when they grew up. He never minded as they were his family and he loved them fiercely. It was much easier for a grown man to stand up to a neurotic and unfeeling mother and their harsh stepfather than let them be bent over with it. The way he had.

He frowned. The light had changed as the sun sank lower in the western sky and caught the shine on a box he'd never seen before. It was wedged low down on the bookcase in front of him and looked like it had been pushed in their in haste. When it had been pushed into placed it had obviously caught on the hanging shimmery cloth draped in front of it and had been prevented from sliding all the way in. Now, it lay half tipped on its side, half in the bookcase and half out.

He sucked in a breath. He knew exactly what it was as when he was younger and his father had been in a good mood, he'd been allowed to sit on the large settee in the formal lounge and open it. He swallowed. When he opened the lid, the tune playing would be London Bridge and his mother's name would be carved inside the wooden lid towards the back. What the hell was Eliza doing with his mother's missing box and why had she hidden it in here?

Suddenly, a cold sweat broke out over him. He knew, and had sensed it the moment he'd seen the incriminating box. Eliza must have pushed it onto the self in a hurry when the plane arrived for her last week and the momentum of the weight of the old documents he knew he'd find in it had toppled it over. He gripped the arms of the chair, willing the sensations of betrayal and pain and nausea to subside. The drone of a plane's engine sounded outside and he recognized the hovering pattern of their pilot as he circled the runway to check for animals on the strip before making his final approach.

Eliza was home. No, not home, not any more, not if what he suspected he'd find in that box proved true. After his father's death, Alex and the solicitor had opened another box that had been in a locked vault. His father's instructions had been clear. In his mother's shiny jewel box which played the tinkling music, he'd left letters to Ben and Amanda and him, to be opened after his death.

He'd said he'd loved the three of them and had wanted to make amends for his harshness in the growing years. The letter had described a man in pain, suffering from his mistakes and regretting many decisions he'd made. It had also told his three children that he had gone to great lengths to heal the breach and rectify any errors made. The problem was that no one knew the location of the mysterious things he'd left behind to fix the Ryan family's problems. Alex guessed that his father would have left precious letters to his children in his mother's old box, as it was a Ryan traditional hiding place, and his father had been a true traditionalist.

It had been then, when the three siblings had searched for the hidden letters and documents that Eliza had announced that the shiny box, as they called it, had been broken beyond repair several month earlier and their father had thrown it into the fire in a fit of pique. The scenario fitted his father's often volatile behavior so closely that no one had questioned her explanation. Ben and Amanda had grieved for the letters, the reconciliation they could never have with their stepfather, even posthumously. He'd also grieved, but in private.

It would have filled a void, an ache in all their souls if they could have had just one letter from their father of remorse, of caring, or of love. And now, sitting before him was the container that had held all their hopes. A stab of pain struck his heart as he also registered what he had pushed out of his mind at the time as ridiculous. Back then, he'd sensed that Eliza was fibbing about the whereabouts of the box. Now, he knew she'd lied. The sunlight's glint from the pretty painted lid mocked her in her absence.

Although, she would walk through that door in a few minutes and if he wanted the proof in his hand before that happened, he needed to move, not sit frozen in disbelief. There would be time later to let the pain wash over him when he had explained her duplicity to her two children. They barely tolerated their mother now, so this would cause them to truly hate her. A hate she probably deserved.

He forced himself to move, to bend, to retrieve the wooden box with its ballet dancers and butterflies and swirls of bright colors decorating the lid. Opening it was harder. He braced for the familiar music. By the time Eliza rushed into the room ten minutes later, he'd scanned the documents and made an assessment and was replaying the tune. His eyes were closed and he'd slumped back into the chair with the box resting on his chest as he let the music drift over him and carry him back to better times.

'How dare you! This is my private room.' She looked at the box and screamed. 'And my private belongings. You've no right to be here, to touch them.'

'Actually, Eliza, I've every right. My mother's box was left to me. It's an antique Russian jewelry box that she brought with her when her family moved from England to Australia when she was ten. It was her prized possession.'

Eliza stepped closer and held out her hand, trying to hide her fury. 'Keep the box then. Just give me the papers from inside it.'

'Ah, yes, the papers. The letters my father wrote to Ben and Amanda explaining that the reason he'd never been able to legally adopt them and give them the Ryan name, was because you were still married to someone else. Isn't that true, Eliza?'

'What does that matter? Your father knew I'd been married before.'

'Yes, but he didn't discover that you'd never been divorced until recently. When he applied for birth certificates and things for your children. All your lies fell apart like a house of cards, didn't they? Was he furious? Did you have another fight? Is that what caused his fatal heart attack? You and your greed and lies?' He stood up from the chair and she sensed his anger and backed away towards the door. 'There were other things in the box, too. It seems you liked to take them out and gloat over them and didn't bother to burn them as you should have.'

'Give them to me! I'll do it now. Nobody else need know.'

'Ha! And do you really imagine that will make up for the harm You've caused so many people. It's all in here, recorded in your hand writing and in your personal diaries. How long did you think you'd get away with it?'

'Forever, you fool,' she screamed, her hand shaking as she pointed her fingers at him. 'You didn't suspect anything in all this time. You, who your father thought was the family genius. The famous doctor, the astute business and cattle man, the wonderful stepbrother. How those stories sickened me when I had to listen to them time after time.'

She laughed, a high pitched and hysterical sound that shot

through his ears and made him shiver. Eliza was unstable. How had he never seen her behavior for what it was before? It seemed so clear now. Her highs and lows, the spending sprees and the obsessions all fitted a pattern of someone with problems.

'We'll get you some professional help. I know a good asylum in Sydney where you'll be very comfortable.'

'Don't be ridiculous! I'm not leaving Undulla after all I've done to stay here.'

She lunged for the box but Alex sidestepped her and moved to the door and passed the box to the person standing there. 'Tommy, did you call the police? And Luke?'

'Yes, they'll be here shortly. I'm so sorry, Alex, for what you've discovered here today.'

'Thanks, Tommy. Although, some of the things I've found here are a help to me, and hopefully to Ben and Amanda.'

He signaled to the other new arrivals to enter and Tommy passed the box over to the police. 'It seems my stepmother's diary is a true account of how she hid the papers that proved she is still married, and not to my father. She committed bigamy in her greed. It also seems that she used many devious methods to rid Undulla of anyone she considered unsuitable. That included my former fiancée as well as the woman I am going to marry. She used Bob to falsify my medical records and pretend that a sperm count had been done, when actually it never had.'

'You stupid fool,' Eliza shrieked again, flying at him in a rage. 'If you hadn't been such as prude, such a nice person, we could have shared Undulla. You forced me to take those actions. How dare you think to bring a woman in here to take my place. I am the true matriarch of the Ryan family.'

'It's a pity that you have no Ryan blood in you then, isn't it? Because my child, my baby...' His breath caught as he said the words for the first time. 'My child is a true Ryan, Eliza. No matter how much you tried, you couldn't prevent me from finding a woman to love and one who is pregnant with my baby.'

Alex stepped forward and patted Luke on the back, mate to mate.

'Luke, I owe you an apology. For a little while there, I actually started to believe that you'd falsified my test results.'

'Alex, Eliza fooled us all. You have nothing to apologize for. Well actually, you do, but not to me. To Kristie for doubting her word. I suggest you get yourself into town as soon as this mess is sorted and go down on your hands and knees and beg her forgiveness.'

'No!' Eliza screamed. 'A Ryan doesn't beg, not ever, not from anyone.'

Alex smiled. 'This Ryan does. I'll do whatever it takes for Kristie to forgive my stupidity. Anything to keep her here in Dinosaur Valley with me where she belongs. Now, Tony, can we take statements or whatever we need to do.'

'Sure, Alex, but I'm afraid it's going to take a while to sort out. I've called for assistance from a legal advisor so we can get a clearer picture of the bigamy side of it, and where Ben and Amanda stand.'

'Ben and Amanda are my siblings. They'll be right here beside me at Undulla for as long we all draw breath.'

'It's good of you to say that, Alex. They'll need a lot of support after what their mother has done to them. Do you want me to ring and tell them, or would you rather do it? Your call.'

'Christ!' Alex closed his eyes and dropped his head as he slumped into his own larger office chair this time.'

'I can tell you that I'm dreading having to do it, but I'm their family so it will be easier coming from me, but thanks for the offer, Tony. Despite knowing Eliza was highly strung, she's still their mother. How do I explain to them that she did all this because she wanted to protect their inheritance?'

Luke had taken Eliza to her bedroom where Peg was assisting her to pack a bag. He'd also given Eliza a sedative to prevent any more hysterical outbursts until they could transport her to a bigger facility for an accurate assessment of her mental status. Tony and his police officers had taken away all the documents to be used as evidence in building their case against Eliza. They all knew she'd probably never stand trial as even in the last hour, her mental insta-bility had worsened. The best thing for her would be a private asylum and Alex would gladly pay to get help for the mother of his brother and sister.

In the end, it had taken them several hours to sort things, notify family members, and search Eliza's room for other evidence. Alex was sick at what they found. It seemed her schemes had been going on for quite some time and nobody had realized until his father had caught her out in the lie about her divorce. From there, it unraveled for Eliza and he suspected the precipitating cause of his father's last heart attack must have been the enormity of what he uncovered in the last week of his life.

To have lived with someone for so long and not have recognized her duplicity must have devastated his proud father. At least Alex could carry out his father's wishes with regards Ben and Amanda's future at Undulla. It would relieve some of their burden to know he'd thought kindly of them and made arrangements for an inheritance for them both, despite discovering they were not even related by marriage to him. For himself, it was a balm to his raw pain to know that in his last weeks of life, their father had been putting his three children's welfare into order, or as much as he could without revealing the entire story.

At last, the work was done at last and he was free to leave but midnight wasn't the correct hour to call on a woman, even a nurse. Tony looked at him over the rim of the glass of rum they were enjoying together to calm his battered nerves.

'Sorry you missed your chance to go into town and see Kristie tonight.'

'It was better to finish things here first anyway, although she'll probably hear the gossip and wonder what's happening. I'll be on the road first thing in the morning though. I have a very important discussion to have with a pregnant lady.'

After Tony left, he was too restless to sleep. Ben and Amanda were coming home in a couple of days and they could commiserate together. Three times he lifted the receiver to dial Kristie's number at the hospital but each time he replaced it with regret. No, she needed her rest.

Tomorrow would be the start of a new chapter for them both, or so he hoped. He prayed he wasn't asking too much from the gods of benevolence by wanting a wife, a baby, and a new future working as a country surgeon. Surely, it was time fate shone brightly on him, on both of them.

He and the woman he loved.

17

Alex drove into the hospital as fast as he dared early the next morning. It reminded him of making the same drive weeks earlier when Kristie had first rung about Wilhelm's disappearing body. So much had happened since then, some good and some bad.

The good was every moment he'd spent with Kristie. The bad was the destruction of what he'd considered his family but, despite Eliza's treachery, he'd keep Ben and Amanda in his life and on Undulla. He was determined to build a stronger relationship with the woman he loved, because he did love Kristie Donaldson and he intended to tell her, often, and for the rest of their lives. Right after he apologized for her doubting her word.

Striding down the corridors, he searched for Mike, relieved when he found him alone in his office. 'Mike, I'm so glad you're back. Tell me everything.'

Mike grinned and admitted, 'It's good to be back. Things seem to have been hopping while we've been away. After you rang this morning, Jenny went crazy interrogating Maxine and Mary and anyone else she could corner. You know how she hates being left out of the loop—'

A loud chuckle sounded from the doorway and both men turned to greet a grinning Jenny. She bounced in wearing purple joggers, pink socks and shorts with an orange polo shirt and kissed Alex's cheek. When she slid onto Mike's lap, Alex shook his head in amusement.

'Jenny, I see being married hasn't improved your dress sense.'

An unrepentant Jenny kissed her husband on the mouth and said to Alex, 'No, but other things have definitely improved with practice.' Mike's smirk was so self-satisfied, and his wandering hands were all over Jenny's body so much that it was embarrassing.

Alex groaned. 'If you two love birds could stop groping each other for a minute, I'm here because I need your help.' He spent the next ten minutes explaining what he'd found hidden in Eliza's room and all the evil she'd done in the Ryan name.

'Alex, we'll do anything to get you together with Kristie. Everybody is upset about what's been happening. I can't believe Eliza lied to you about everything.'

Alex signaled to Mike and he understood. Pushing her to her feet, he asked his wife, 'Jenny, can you find out where she is now? Nobody seems to know where she's gone.'

'You got the wrong end of the stick in Brisbane, but I thought Kristie would have confided in you by now.'

'She said that she couldn't break your confidences without your permission.'

Mike smiled. 'That's Kristie. Loyal to a fault.'

'Okay, so if you and Kristie have never been more than friends, what is going on? Why was she kissing you like that the morning after your wedding?'

'Kristie and I became friends when our brothers—'

'Your brother Brendon? The one with the drug problem.'

'Yeah, and Kristie's brother Steven has the same problem. They developed schizophrenia from taking drugs and ended up in a mental hospital at the same time. They became friends, so when they were to go to a low-key drug rehabilitation unit, Kristie and I pulled stings to get them sent to the hospital where we worked. That way we could keep an eye on them. I barely knew Kristie until then, though we worked at the same hospital and lived in the same neighborhood.'

'I assumed you and Kristie had some sort of past together that she didn't want me, or Jenny, to know about.'

'No, I told Jenny right from the start about Brendon's problems, but Kristie and I had a pact that no one else would know. It was to protect the boys until they cleaned up their acts. Kristie always wanted to move to a small town so Steven could get a fresh start.'

'Why didn't she?'

'Because of her mother.'

'She told me her mother died a year ago from cancer.'

'But I bet she didn't tell you that she nursed her at home for as long as possible so that she could keep Steven at home with them. She fought hard to keep Steven from permanent hospitalization and for her mother to stay at home as long as possible. For the last two months, her mother lived in a care home because Kristie had to work to pay the rent.'

'I wish she'd told me the whole story.'

'She was always very proud. Too proud to accept help.'

'Except for you?'

'We shared family with the same problems. It made us close, closer than normal friends, but it was never anything more. In all the time I knew her, Kristie was too busy with her other responsibilities to even have a boyfriend.'

'She'd had one though, earlier.'

Mike's shrewd look made Alex redden but he wasn't about to spill any pillow talk revelations.

'She told me about him. The guy sounds like slime.'

'We agree on that. When things got tough for Kristie, he baled. Broke off their engagement. Said he didn't want to spend years waiting for her to be rid of her family problems.'

'Definite slime. Though I screwed up too when I accused her of being with you, or someone else.'

'Because of Eliza.'

'My scheming stepmother, or rather the woman who pretended

to marry my father, convinced me that I was sterile. But damn it, I still can't believe I was so gullible. So stupid.'

'Alex, don't be too hard on yourself. When you arrived back in the valley, you were a mess. You had enough on your plate with your best friend being killed and Monica deserting you and then your father's death.'

'I even denied the baby is mine.'

'So do your believe it now?'

'I don't need to wait for the results of my test in Emerald. I knew that I was only the second man she'd been with and Eliza spelt out in her diary how she'd used Bob to change my hospital reports, and later to remove them. I'd seen the chart earlier, read it, and believed that I was sterile. Eliza counted on the fact that I've always preached protection to Ben and Amanda and she assumed that I'd do the same myself, no matter what the circumstances. But then, I met Kristie and threw all my own rules out the window.'

Mike looked at Alex with pity. 'Mate, you've really made a mess of this. You should have known Kristie is trustworthy after the time you spent with her in Brisbane. Or even from the fact that she's my best friend. Did you really think I'd be friends with a money chasing woman?'

'Of course not. I should have trusted my instincts all along and believed in our relationship. When she came here, all she wanted was chance to explain and to go back to what we had.'

'From what Jenny could find out around here, Kristie came here because she's still in love with you. And now we know she's carrying your child.'

Alex felt wrecked. Last night had been hell on wheels. He'd rid Undulla of Eliza's presence but had to explain to Ben and Amanda what their mother had done. In trying to secure their inheritance rights for Undulla, she'd nearly destroyed his life. He understood her being ambitious for her children, yet the damage she'd done to everyone was unforgivable.

Mike's phone rang and Alex wandered over to the window, listening with half an ear to one side of what was obviously a heated conversation. Mike grunted, groaned, and fired off rapid questions. With a stunned look, he hung up the phone.

'That was Steven, Kristie's brother. He's here in town, at the bus stop.'

'Here? Did Kristie know he was coming?'

'He wanted to surprise her but she isn't answering her phone. I'm going to pick him up.'

'No, I'll go. I need to talk to him.'

'Ah, Alex, There's something else you need to know. He's not alone.'

Alex drove to the bus depot at the information centre and parked his truck close by, although he'd already picked out Kristie's brother. He had the same look and the same smile. He was leaning down to speak to the young girl sitting on a dinosaur seat and holding a new baby close to her chest. Her shoulders were drooped with exhaustion and the baby was whimpering and squirming.

Alex grinned. Yep, their life was complicated but he welcomed this sort of complication. Family, babies, and all it involved. And a life working in medicine. He strode forward and introduced himself, though Steven already knew who he was and his initial greeting was wary.

Alex couldn't blame him after the way he'd treated Steven's sister but he would make it up to them all. Not caring who was watching, Alex hugged Steven's girlfriend and took the baby from her, expertly putting it over his shoulder and rubbing its back. This would be good practice for their own baby, he decided with a huge smile. When all the formalities were finished, Alex drove the new little family group to the hospital to find Kristie. Steven eyed him warily, but that was okay. He deserved some reserve after his behavior and he already felt a bond with Steven and hoped they could be friends, and brothers-in-law, once he convinced Kristie to marry him.

'Jenny, where is she?' Her worried expression frightened Alex. 'What's wrong?'

Jenny bit her lip. 'Alex, she's gone.'

'Gone. What do you mean gone?'

'Max helped her pack her car. She took everything and drove out nearly an hour ago.'

'Where was she going?'

'She's staying in Longreach tonight and then going on to the coast tomorrow.'

'She left without saying goodbye? No, I won't let it happen again. She belongs here with me.'

Jenny clasped Alex's hand but he pulled away and turned to the door. She nodded understanding. 'Go! Catch up to her.'

'I'm going to convince her to come back.'

18

Alex was certain of what he wanted for the first time in many weeks. Certain of what he needed, or rather, who he needed. With a determined stride, he headed to the car park. Now he just had to hope he could catch up to Kristie before she went too far out of his life because the idea of living without her appalled him. He'd go down on his hands and knees to beg her forgiveness if that's what it took.

He drove through town and turned onto the highway towards the coast with his mind racing. If she'd already reached Longreach, he'd drive up and down every street and past every hotel until he found her and if that didn't work, he'd throw himself upon the mercy of the local police. If he looked half as bad on the outside as he felt on the inside, he hoped they'd feel sorry enough for him that they'd assist in his quest. True love could bring out the romantic in even the toughest of men.

Thirty minutes later, on one the long stretches of road the bush was famous for, he spotted a vehicle half a kilometer ahead. The car was pulled to the side of the road with its bonnet raised as steam billowed from the engine and hovered in the hot air. His gut tightened as he realized it was Kristie's broken down car and he couldn't see a driver.

For a moment, he panicked as he knew only too well that a solitary woman on a deserted road was easy pickings for any deviant or criminal cruising past. Oh, please God, please let her be all right, he chanted. When he noticed a figure slumped over on a grassy slope under a shady tree not far from the car, relief overwhelmed him.

Even so, the last hundred meters felt endless as he pulled near enough to see if she was injured. Kristie's head was down on her knees and as he pulled his truck over in front of her dusty car and he could barely draw breath. He sent up fervent prayers that she and their baby were safe, unharmed.

Kristie was alerted to someone's presence by the sound of an engine passing by her steaming car. Dragging herself from her gloom, she swiped at her tears and lifted her head to see who'd stopped. She should feel concerned about sitting by herself on a lonely road but truth to tell, she was beyond caring. Her nerves were stretched to the limit of endurance and her hormones were running amuck. Even raising her head took a huge effort.

The driver's door slammed and the man walked towards her car. Her watery gaze connected with his, and she gasped at the welcome sight. Alex, tall, stunning and wonderful. Cattle baron, doctor, father to be. He jogged along the road, and then picking up pace and running as fast as his injured leg would allow. Without a word, he dropped to the ground beside her and scooped her into his lap to bury his face in her disheveled curls.

Clasped tightly to his chest, she inhaled the familiar smell of him. Her body shook under the onslaught of emotions but he soothed her tremors, snuggled her closer and caressed her back as if he intended holding her this way forever. The masculine aroma and heat rising from him was a familiar comfort and she loved it, loved him, and wanted to wallow in it forever.

She lifted her mouth and pressed her lips to his, encouraging him to kiss her in that way he had where all her childhood fantasies came to life. She was a princess being embraced by her knight in shining armor. The fact that he'd ridden in, not on a shining white steed but a grimy red truck made no difference. All that mattered was that her hero had come to rescue her.

For the first time in her life, she felt truly safe and sheltered, yet part of her couldn't trust what was happening because she'd been let down by men so many times before. By her father, her ex fiancée, and then Alex when he denied that her baby was his. Perhaps trusting wholeheartedly was going to be beyond her. Yet, in Alex's arms, she yearned to let go of her fears and let his protection cloak her. She longed to be cherished. She lifted her head and stared at him in wonder.

'What are you doing here?'

'I'm holding the woman I love and I'm never going to let her go.'

Her heart raced and her breath caught at the words he hadn't spoken to her since the night of Mike and Jenny's wedding. During the past two months, she'd ached to hear him say them again.

'You...you love me?'

His face remained pressed to her neck, but she felt his nod. He seemed lost and vulnerable and she'd never seen him like this before. Alex was normally so self-contained and capable that as she'd driven away from the valley, she'd imagined him going on with his life and wiping her from his thoughts without much fuss. But as he watched her now, she saw that his eyes were damp with tears.

'Sweetheart, I love you so much. I won't let you leave because I need you and the valley needs you.'

She snorted in disbelief. 'The hospital board gave me my marching orders, thanks to Eliza. They wanted me out of their town as fast as possible, because an unmarried mother is too distressing for their lofty moralists.'

'But you won't be unwed, because you'll be married to me.'

'Alex, we've been over this. You don't even believe the baby is yours.'

'I do. I truly do. And I'm sorrier than I can ever say that I ever doubted you.'

'Tell me truthfully, is this because you got the results of your test back?'

'No, I haven't seen the results and I don't need to. I know you don't lie and you don't sleep around and I was a blind fucking idiot for suggesting such a thing.'

She placed a finger over his lips. 'Shush. It doesn't matter now.'

'It does matter because I've made a mess of everything. It's a long story, but last night I confronted Eliza and she admitted that she'd lied. I'd accepted everything she said because I felt guilty about my father. He wanted me home years ago, yet every year I made excuses until it was too late. My accident sent me back to Undulla, but I was too late because my father had already died. Eliza knew which buttons to press to get me to do what she wanted. But she's gone, Kristie, sent away from Undulla and never to return. I'm going to fix us, I swear.'

'I meant it when I said it doesn't matter. I fell in love with you in Brisbane. I loved you when I swallowed my pride and came here, even though I knew a modern woman isn't supposed to chase a man. I did it anyway and do you want to know why?'

'Why?'

'Because I believed in us enough to know we were meant to be together. We're too strong and too smart to let anything, or anyone, keep us apart.'

'I didn't have your faith and I let you down.'

'You've never let me down. That night in the pub, you came through for us. You stood up and told everyone the baby was yours. That I was yours. Alex, I loved you when you were a city doctor and I love you as a cattle man, but most of all, I wanted a chance to love you when you're a father to our baby.'

She took his hand and placed it over her stomach where a new life grew, a Ryan to carry on the name. 'For this baby, and for all the next ones, I want you.'

'To think that I nearly lost you again. You nearly left town.'

'Ah, about that.' She threw back her head and laughed.

'What?'

'I told everyone I was only going as far as Longreach. I even told them which pub I was staying at.'

'Yeah, so?'

'I think that subconsciously I hoped they'd tell you where I'd be. Deep down, I still prayed that you'd come after me and stop me from leaving.'

'Sweetheart, I may have been slow on the uptake, but I know now what I want and I'll always come after you.'

'Even when I mess up and lose bodies?'

'Especially then. It's the most entertainment the town's had in years. And by the way, the case has been solved.'

'They found out what happened to Wilhelm?'

He laughed. 'Yes. When the autopsy was finally done it showed that he died from a tumor, not the poison his poor wife thought she'd given him by mistake. What he took was very, very weak. It didn't kill him, but his family panicked and thought that she'd be thrown into jail. They took the body and hid it, thinking if they waited long enough it would be too late to prosecute their grandmother. The town's gone crazy with that juicy bit of gossip.'

'Well,' she said, her wandering hands leaving him in no doubt of her meaning, 'I suggest we give the town something more to gossip about. Right here, right now.'

He looked up and down the deserted road, knowing that any time soon a car would come along. 'It's rather shocking to be risking the Ryan family reputation in such a lewd fashion on the side of a road.' Then he grinned, that sexy boyish smile that made her heart stutter and she knew it'd be okay. They'd make up their own rules for behavior and the valley moralists would have to make up new rules to keep up with them.

'Why not? After all, we're an old married—'

'We aren't married.'

'Before this week is out, we will be.' She started to argue but he silenced her with a kiss. Then another, and another until they were sprawled on the grassy hillock in plain view of the world and they didn't care.

'I want to put an overseer on Undulla so I can go back to work. What do you think?'

'I think it's wonderful news. Where are you going to practice?'

'In the valley and I'll visit other district hospitals regularly and do their surgeries.'

'Will that be enough of a challenge for you?'

He laughed. 'If I want more challenges, I'll make more babies with you. And I'll manage Undulla on a part-time basis until Ben and Amanda want to come home, although I'm not going to pressure them like my father did. Guilt over Undulla nearly ruined my life and I don't want it to ruin theirs.'

'Oh, Alex, it sounds wonderful.'

'Oh, and by the way, it seems our family is growing faster than we thought.'

She automatically looked down at her stomach and rubbed her hand over her small, rounded lump, giving him a puzzled look.

Alex laughed again. 'No, not that family. Your brother has arrived in town, along with his partner, soon to be wife, and your most adorable baby niece.'

She clapped her hands over her mouth. 'Oh, my goodness. But will you mind having so much family now after being more or less alone for so long?'

'No, I'll love having everyone around. And it seems Steven has a hankering to become a cattle hand, so perhaps he'll like living at Undulla. Now, Kristie, my darling, I'm letting you up from this patch of grass until you promise to marry me, and soon. Repeat after me, I love you, Alex Ryan and yes, I will marry you.'

She might not have said those exact words, but neither of them cared when she showed him rather cheekily what she was thinking. She raced to his truck, climbed onto the back seat, and waggled a finger at him. 'Come and make me, Doctor Ryan.'

He was slow and stupid before where this woman was concerned, but he'd never make that mistake again. He chased her to the truck and leaned over her, pinning her squirming body to the seat under him.

'Nurse Donaldson, soon to be Nurse Ryan, you and our baby are the most important things in the world to me.' He looked her straight in the face. 'I love you both. Forever and a day.'

She closed her eyes and silently thanked fate for choosing this day to make her car engine overheat and for giving them another chance. They had what they'd both wanted most in life.

Love, and family, and a wonderful town to live and work in.

EXCERPT KELLY'S JUSTICE

I lived in Vanuatu, previously the New Hebrides, in the South Pacific for nine years and loved the island life and its fascinating history. Loving Lady Katharine is set in historic Vanuatu and my contemporary military suspense, Kelly's Justice, is set in contemporary Vanuatu. I hope you enjoy reading both versions of Vanuatu.

San Diego, U.S.A.

Kelly, codename Riddles, listened to Marci's briefing in the community room at the compound in San Diego. When her new boss, an ex-Navy Seal, visited Kelly in Australia and invited her to join a new international security team, Kelly didn't hesitate as Marci had top level clearance with many organizations and accepted both government and private contracts.

The whole team was at this meeting, a group of well-trained and feisty women Riddles would trust with her life, and would die trying to protect each and every one of them. Using Marci's inherited money, their amazing compound was set up with a training course, top notch IT equipment and every weapon they would ever need. Plus a bomb making area well enough equipped to keep Dee busy, and happy.

Kelly lived off compound so she could continue teaching classes in martial arts and hand-to-hand fighting, but like every team member she also had a fantastic apartment within the compound. And like every other team member, she'd left her old life behind and deliberately disconnected from the people she'd known in the Australian army and in her personal life.

This was an exciting opportunity. A new country and a new life, yet a place where she could utilize all her old military skills and do the thing she loved most, fight for justice.

She'd been brought up by grandparents who had strong moral and social beliefs and she'd adopted those same attitudes. Help keep people safe from the evils of society and ensure that those who broke the law and endangered lives were captured and put behind bars. Her grandparents might not be with her any longer, but by working with Marci and the team, she helped remove many of the world's most dangerous scumbags from the streets, permanently, and she knew her grandparents would feel proud of the person she'd become.

"Five teens," Marci said, "were taken captive while at a conference, cum working holiday, in a South Pacific country. They were on one of the many islands making up the country of Vanuatu, previously called the New Hebrides. Three of the teenagers are American and two Australian, so a multinational group has been asked to help. Specifically us, as we fit the description and we have high level clearances for international incidents that need our skills."

Hallie asked the pressing question they all wanted answered. "Any ransom demands yet?"

Marci shook her head. "No demands, and we currently have no idea why they were taken, or who is holding them. Hard to imagine that a group of teenagers learning about the societies and cultures of the South Pacific would have deliberately caused any trouble. Vanuatu is a peaceful country with very little crime or violence. The locals live an idyllic lifestyle. Beaches, fishing, gardens for food. But we do know that drug traffickers have made several attempts to use those islands to hide drug shipments. A half-way storage spot between Hawaii and Australia. It's possible these kids stumbled across something. Saw something they shouldn't have and were taken as leverage."

Marci shrugged. "So far, all we know is that five teenagers have disappeared. No ransom requests, although one of the Americans comes from a wealthy family. Mother is a senator and father is from a family with old money, and plenty of it. All families have been notified and we're waiting to hear re any demands, although most of the parents currently see this as a case of teenagers playing tourist and getting lost. The Senator, being much more security aware, is expecting a ransom demand. If that happens, negotiators will step in. Meanwhile, the senator is funding a multinational team to locate and, if possible, extract the group."

She looked around the group. "I know this isn't our normal sort of mission, but my contact in Washington, General Craig Simmons, recommended us for the job. He and the Senator know each other well and she personally asked me for our help. In case this is a false alarm, she wants a team who can slip quietly into Vanuatu, keep their presence very low key, and disappear if the teens turn up by themselves. People who know how to avoid attention, but with high enough clearance to go into Vanuatu armed. People like us."

She nodded towards Kelly. "Riddles, you're the ideal person to go in first and do some recon. At the moment, we're going in blind and we need someone who knows the culture on the ground in a hurry. I'm sending Jacky with you and, if necessary, a larger team can be right on your heels. Do you want to explain to those not in the know why I am sending you, specifically, to the South Pacific?"

Kelly nodded. "I worked in Vanuatu for six months as part of an Australian army initiative to find, and shut down, any would-be drug routes or potential traffickers. At the time, there was strong intel that Vanuatu had been chosen as an ideal place for drug drop off and storage because the locals are known for their laid-back attitude, and their acceptance of foreigners on their islands. And because of the constant traffic of boats, ships and even yachts between Vanuatu and Australia, there were plenty of opportunities to hide drugs aboard any of these vessels."

"Did you find routes? Traffickers?" Marci asked. Her boss's questions were always direct, and her knowledge of countries and world politics was staggering. She had her finger on the pulse of major conflicts all over the place and for what she didn't know, she requested information from one of her many well-placed and high-ranking contacts.

Her private task force was often requested for high profile cases because Marci was efficient, proficient, and caring, a great combination in Kelly's eyes. If Marci wanted Riddles in the South Pacific, their boss had a good reason. If she was also sending Jacky, Marci expected more face-to-face clashes than weapon use as both she and Jacky were the most proficient at close up fighting.

As Marci recruited each of the eleven women for her group, she'd promised that when the time was right every resource would be employed to solve whatever personal difficulty had driven each woman to accept Marci's invitation. Right now, their team hackers were tracking the illegal activities of Kelly's ex-boyfriend, Ronnie, and trying to establish which of Ronnie's army mates were involved in his illegal activities. Which men had assisted Ronnie when he accused her personally of cheating and professionally of selling information on the black market?

If she could prove that Ronnie and his mystery partners had framed her, she could set the record straight and finally clear her name. When the blot on her record was expunged, she'd forget her relationship with Ronnie and the callous way he'd treated her and concentrate on this new and exciting phase of her life. Once the truth was revealed, she could go home and visit her family with her head held high, instead of feeling ashamed that she'd failed in her army career. Her new motto was *out with the bad and in with the good.*

"Yes, lots of routes." Kelly said. "And lots of traffickers, though no arrests of the major players in Vanuatu itself, but there were arrests later in Australia and the U.S. And in three Asian countries, watch and wait orders at the time led to the dispersal of several smaller groups within the next six months. Drug traffickers do not like being watched, especially in S.E. Asia. Once they know the authorities have their eyes on them, they disperse and move on. It doesn't stop determined players, but jails in Asian countries are notoriously overcrowded and no small-time player will take that risk. Closing them down isn't as good as arrests but the more groups we can shut down, the better. The local police in Vanuatu were naive when it came to drugs when we arrived. Not so much by the time we left. We were hopeful that with better surveillance, some of the drug boats could be identified and then Australian customs would seize the drugs on arrival in Australia."

"Do you think these kidnappings could be to do with drug trafficking?"

"Could be," Kelly said with a shrug. "The usual place to store drugs was a remote shed or house, somewhere away from the local people. Away from the well-beaten tracks that crisscrossed between villages. If these kids stumbled across an old building and noticed something unusual, extra security, vehicles coming and going, they might have poked their noses into something dangerous and found themselves in a whole lot of trouble."

"What do you think will happen to the kids if traffickers have them?"

Kelly frowned. "Depends how desperate these people are, and how ruthless. Vanuatu isn't known for hard core crime, but if drug traffickers have the kids, they'll need to stop them mouthing off to the authorities. I can't see them releasing them alive, even if they ask for a ransom."

Marci said, "We're hoping to hear soon which island the kids are being held on. But we can't wait for that information. I want two of you in the air before then. A larger group will follow when we have more intel. If this is a simple extraction of five kids, Kelly, you might have a chance to get in and get them out quickly. However, the higher ups fear a worse scenario. Chatter on the net suggests a large shipment of drugs is on its way to Australia via either Fiji or Vanuatu. Worth millions. Which means we'll be dealing with a well-organized group rather than a small-time operation. And that puts those kids in a lot more danger."

Kelly and Jacky touched down at the main airport in the early hours of the morning, the jet landing smoothly and taxiing towards the airport buildings.

"You okay, Kelly," Jacky asked with a frown. "You didn't get much sleep."

"Yeah, I'm good. Brings back a lot of memories coming back to Port Vila."

"Good or bad?"

"Bit of both, I guess. I loved the place and the people, but I was here when I found out for certain that my ex had betrayed me. Personally, and professionally."

"What did he do?"

She didn't get to answer as the pilots left the cockpit and walked up to them. "There are three men in the airport waiting for you. Marci said there is updated intel and these guys have been working here for the last two weeks, following a strong lead on a drug route. They'll fill you in."

As they walked down the steps, three men walked out of the airport and strode towards them. Kelly stopped so suddenly that Jacky ran into her back.

"What's wrong?" Jacky's gaze flicked to the men now waiting for them at the wire boundary fence. "Riddles, you look like you've seen a ghost. I'm guessing that you know them."

ABOUT THE AUTHOR

Tag Line - Making history fun, one year at a time.

I now live in a sunny part of Australia after spending many years in developing countries in the South Pacific. I love traveling, anywhere and everywhere, meeting crazy characters, and visiting the Australian outback.

My sexy heroes and feisty heroines challenge tradition, and though they might live a privileged life, they also understand the seamier parts of life.

I can be found in many Facebook groups talking about books and history and am always busy on Twitter, Instagram, and my personal favorite, Pinterest.

To learn more about Suzi Love and my new releases, join my newsletter at my suzilove.com. I am on Instagram and Goodreads and have lots of Pinterest Boards as suziloveoz. And please join my Facebook Group, Suzi Love's Lovelies, to keep up with my news on books and history.

Please visit my WEBSITE
Email me: suzi@suzilove.com

BOOKS BY SUZI LOVE

Fiction By Suzi Love

Embracing Scandal Book 1 Scandalous Siblings Series

Scenting Scandal Book 2 Scandalous Siblings Series

December Scandal Book 3 Scandalous Siblings Series

The Viscount's Pleasure House Book 1 Irresistible Aristocrats

Four Times A Virgin Book 2 Irresistible Aristocrats

Petunia and the Pearl Diver

Love After Waterloo

Pleasure House Ball

Kelly's Justice group Book 4

Outback Arrival

Loving Lady Katharine Book 3 Irresistible Aristocrats

Old Sydney Town

Non-Fiction By Suzi Love

History Of Christmases Past Book 1 History Events

Easter In Images Book 2 History Events

History of Valentine's Day

Regency Overview Book 1 Regency Life Series

Young Gentleman's Day Book 2 Regency Life Series

Older Gentleman's Day Book 3 Regency Life Series

Young Lady's Day Book 4 Regency Life Series

Older Lady's Day Book 5 Regency Life Series

Self Publishing: Absolute Beginners Guide.

HISTORY NOTES SERIES

Here are some of the many titles in this Non-Fiction History Series.

20 History Notes Corsets 1880-1900
21 History Notes Corsets Early 1900s
22 History Notes Corsets Box Set
23 History Notes Fashion Men 1800-1819
24 History Notes Fashion Women Box Set
25 History Notes Fashion Women 1801-1804
26 History Notes Fashion Women 1805-1809
27 History Notes Fashion Women 1810-1814
28 History Notes Fashion Women 1815-1819
Coming Soon:-
History Notes Underwear
History Notes Grand Tour
History Notes Mail Deliveries
History Notes Peerage
History Notes Food
History Notes Carriages
History Notes Money
History Notes Sewing
History Notes Hats
History Notes Mourning
History Notes Furniture
History Notes Shoes
History Notes Trades
History Notes Clubs
History Notes Fans
History Notes Sports
Historic London
Overview
Bridges
Hospitals
Churches
Famous

REVIEWS

Reviews are like gold to authors. I would appreciate it if you could leave a review, good or bad, for this book at any book retailer.

And don't forget, to get insider news about my book releases, any discounted books or contests that I am a part of, you should sign up for my newsletter. I promise you will only ever hear from me when I have exciting news, about me or my other author friends. www.-suzilove.com

You can send me an email : suzi@suzilove.com.

Or send a letter : Suzi Love, 258/ 52 University Way, Sippy Downs, Queensland, 4556, Australia.

www.ingramcontent.com/pod-product-compliance
Lightning Source LLC
Chambersburg PA
CBHW070024260626
47159CB00005B/1944